© Stephen Mitchelmore

About the Author

GABRIEL JOSIPOVICI was born in Nice in 1940 of Russo-Italian, Romano-Levantine parents. He lived in Egypt from 1945 to 1956, when he moved to the United Kingdom. He read English at St. Edmund Hall, Oxford, and graduated in 1961. From 1963 to 1996, he taught at the University of Sussex, where he is now a research professor in the Graduate School of Humanities.

He has published more than a dozen novels, three volumes of short stories, and a number of critical books. His plays have been performed throughout Britain, France, and Germany, and his work has been translated into the major European languages and into Arabic. In 2001 he published *A Life*, a memoir/biography of his mother, the translator and poet Sacha Rabinovitch. His most recent novels are *Everything Passes* and *Only Joking*.

Goldberg: Variations

Also by Gabriel Josipovici

Fiction
The Inventory (1968)
Words (1971)
Mobius the Stripper: Stories and Short Plays (1974)
The Present (1975)
Four Stories (1977)
Migrations (1977)
The Echo Chamber (1979)
The Air We Breathe (1981)
Conversations in Another Room (1984)
Contre-jour: A Triptych after Pierre Bonnard (1984)
In the Fertile Land (1987)
Steps: Selected Fiction and Drama (1990)
The Big Glass (1991)
In a Hotel Garden (1993)
Moo Pak (1995)
Now (1998)
Only Joking (2006)
Everything Passes (2006)

Theater
Mobius the Stripper (1974)
Vergil Dying (1977)

Nonfiction
The World and the Book (1971, 1979)
The Modern English Novel: The Reader, the Writer and the Book
(ed.) (1975)
The Lessons of Modernism (1977, 1987)
The Sirens' Song: Selected Essays of Maurice Blanchot (ed.) (1980)
Writing and the Body (1982)
The Mirror of Criticism: Selected Reviews (1983)
The Book of God: A Response to the Bible (1988, 1990)
Text and Voice: Essays 1981–1991 (1992)
A Life (2001)
The Singer on the Shore (2006)

Goldberg: Variations

Gabriel Josipovici

ecco
7

HARPER PERENNIAL

NEW YORK • LONDON • TORONTO • SYDNEY

HARPER ● PERENNIAL

First published in Great Britain in 2002 by Carcanet Press Limited.

HarperCollins books may be purchased for educational, business, or sales promotional use. For information please write: Special Markets Department, HarperCollins Publishers, 10 East 53rd Street, New York, NY 10022.

First Harper Perennial edition published 2007.

Library of Congress Cataloging-in-Publication data is available on request.

ISBN: 978-0-06-089723-9 (pbk.)
ISBN-10: 0-06-089723-6 (pbk.)

07 08 09 10 11 ❖/RRD 10 9 8 7 6 5 4 3 2 1

In memory of my aunt, Chickie Baiocchi, 1909–2000

Contents

Goldberg: Variations

1. Goldberg

We arrived at nightfall. Mr Hammond set me down at the manor and drove on to see his son. Mr Westfield was expecting me. His manservant showed me to my room. It is larger than our living-room and has a small bathroom attached, the whole elegantly panelled and freshly painted. The windows are large and look directly down on to the kitchen garden, but the big oak and elm trees of the park are visible beyond. It is altogether very pleasant and peaceful, and I am sure I will be able to do very good work here. There is a desk in one corner and Mr Westfield has provided me with every kind of paper, pencil, pen and ink.

I was given dinner in a little room adjoining the main dining-room. It was very abundant and well-cooked, with a bottle of excellent wine to go with it, and coffee to follow. This I declined, and asked instead for a cup of lemon verbena tea such as I am accustomed to at home, but this the maid could not provide. She promised, however, to fetch in a supply on the morrow, and furnished me instead with a cup of rosehip tea, pleasant to the taste though a little tart.

At nine o'clock I was ushered into Mr Westfield's rooms. He was lying on a chaise-longue, drinking coffee. He is a large, pleasant-faced man, florid in complexion and with a conspicuous wart on his nose. I did not like to tell him at this juncture that his problems might be eased if he did not drink coffee after six o'clock in the evening. He has presumably already been told this by his physician and chosen to disregard it.

I am to read to him till dawn or else till I am sure he is asleep, whichever is the first. I am to sit in the room adjacent to the bedroom, the very room where I had my first interview with him, in a chair close to the door leading into the bedroom, which will be open. Only when he begins to snore am I to stop. Steady, heavy breathing does not mean that he is asleep. Indeed, he points out that this would be the very worst moment to stop, as the sudden silence would immediately catapult him into wakefulness, even if he had been on the point of falling asleep.

I asked if he wished to hear me read, but he said he had made enquiries and had every confidence in my abilities. He wants an even tone of voice, but not monotonous. Do not try to read as though you were soothing me to sleep, he told me. I cannot abide that. Read in your normal manner, but do not let yourself be carried away by what you are reading. Only if I am compelled to attend will I be able to forget my own thoughts for long enough to fall asleep.

With that he dismissed me, instructing me to return with my book at midnight. I asked him if I should knock and he pondered a moment, then said that I should. However, he himself would not reply. Knock merely and then let yourself in, he said. The door will not be locked.

His room was in darkness when I returned, but he called out to me from his bed, and when I answered he asked me to be seated and to begin when I was ready. I settled myself in the chair, adjusted the lamp, and began. But after a while he called out to me again and asked me to enter the bedroom. The light from the lamp allowed me to make out the large four-poster in which I presumed he lay. I stood at the door, but his voice, coming from the recess of the bed, asked me to come forward and to sit at his bedside. When I had done this he lay for so long in silence I thought my simple presence there beside him had been enough to do what all the skills of my delivery had so far failed to do, but eventually he spoke, very softly, and asked me about you and the children. I answered all his questions as simply and clearly as I was able. He asked me then whether I myself had anything written I might choose to read from instead of the books I had brought with me. I answered that I had much, but not with me. I wondered whether he would suggest sending a servant to fetch these the next day, but he lay in silence for a while, and then asked whether

I would be prepared to write some special thing to read to him, night after night.

– What kind of thing do you have in mind? I asked him.

He laughed at that, and said he was not himself a writer, and that he would leave such things to me. I understood the reason then for the desk under the window and the different kinds of paper and pen laid out upon it. I said I would try.

– I will not have anything other than a new composition of your own, he said.

He was silent again, and I wondered what I should do. Did he wish me to return to the other room and take up my reading again, or leave him altogether, or else to sit there in case he had other questions for me to answer. I was debating these different possibilities when he said:

– I have read all the books that have been written, Mr Goldberg, and it makes me melancholy. A terrible tedium comes upon me whenever I open again one of these volumes, or even when another voice renders me their contents.

– But would not a new book arouse your interest too much? I asked him, would it not have the effect of keeping you awake rather than the desired one of sending you to sleep?

– My friend, he said, you speak without thought. A new story, a story which is really new and really a story, will give the person who reads or hears it the sense that the world has become alive again for him. I would put it like this: the world will start to breathe for him where before it had seemed as if made of ice or rock. And it is only in the arms of that which breathes that we can fall asleep, for only then are we confident that we will ourselves wake up alive. Am I not right, my friend?

I agreed with him at once. I told him that I had not thought in those terms before, but that now he had put it in this way I could see the rightness of his proposition.

– My friend, he said, you had no need to see it in these terms. You are a writer, not a thinker. I, alas, am a thinker. That is why you can sleep but I cannot.

After that he was silent again, and for so long that I made a movement to rise from my chair. But as I did so he spoke again.

– No, he said. Stay where you are. Tonight we will talk. Tomorrow you will read to me from your new work.

I wondered then at the boldness of his assumption that I could in a day produce enough matter to read from the following night from midnight till the coming of the dawn. I did not like to raise false expectations in his breast, but likewise I did not, at that moment, wish to rouse him by challenging his assumption. He spoke quietly, and was clearly in a kind of half-sleep, from which it was my duty to lead him rather in the direction of slumber than to arouse him to full wakefulness.

He asked me then again about you, and whether we minded being thus kept apart for a period of days if not of weeks.

– A poor author, sir, I said to him, cannot always do what his family would like.

– But if you had to choose, he pressed me, between spending the night at your desk or in your bed, which would you choose? I mean, he added, sensing that I had perhaps not wholly understood him, if you had no other time to write but at night?

I pondered the question, for it seemed to me that he was the sort of man who did not care for an unconsidered reply. And as long as he knew that a reply would in fact be forthcoming, he was in no hurry to have it, but would let me take my time, sitting there beside him in the quiet room, with only the light on the desk in the adjoining chamber to keep the darkness at bay.

Eventually I told him what I considered to be the truth, which is that if the choice were for one night only there would be no question of my deciding to spend it in bed with you, but that if he was talking about a permanent state of affairs the choice would be more difficult.

– Let us say, my friend, he said, that financial considerations do not enter into the equation.

– You are, sir, I said, asking a philosopher's question.

– My friend, he said, what other kind can a philosopher ask?

– My answer would still be the same, I said. I trust, though, I added, that it would not come to such a choice.

– But if it were to? he pressed me.

– Not to lie in bed next to the wife I love would make my life hardly worth living, I said to him. Not to write as I wish would have the same effect. You would condemn me by your insistence that I choose.

– Could you not lie with your wife and compose as you do so? he asked me.

I told him that the difference between composing in your head and on paper was like that between embracing a ghost and a person of flesh and blood. He seemed to understand, for he was silent then. Once again I felt that he had perhaps finally succumbed to sleep but once again, as I moved my chair, his voice came to me out of the recesses of the bed.

– Perhaps, he said, that is the difference between a philosopher and a writer.

I waited for him to continue but he was silent again for a long while. Eventually, though, he continued.

– It is only ghosts we philosophers ever embrace, he said. That is why so many of us suffer from insomnia.

I waited again and again he continued, after a lengthy pause:

– We need to rediscover the living body.

He seemed happy now to talk to himself. He said:

– But even if we did so it would straightway die in our embrace.

I did not think he wanted me to talk, but suddenly he asked me:

– What do you think of us philosophers, my friend?

I told him I did not normally think of them, but that I imagined they were engaged in answering the most important questions of existence.

– Do not stop there, my friend, he said. There is no need to spare me.

I told him I did not understand what he was trying to say.

– We can indeed answer all the central questions of existence, he said, but that is not to say that we have answered anything at all.

– How so? I asked him.

– An answer to a question is an act, not a set of words, he said. That, he added, is why we philosophers lie awake in our beds.

I was silent then, not wishing to agree or disagree with him. Perhaps sensing my dilemma he changed the subject somewhat.

– Why do you think, my friend, he asked me, that your race has produced so few philosophers?

– We have produced more than people imagine, I said.

– Is it, he said, because it is a race which relies for its self-definition so much upon memory?

I was impressed by the acuteness of his understanding. – Do you know much about our race? I asked him.

– Only what I read, he said. There is precious little opportunity to study the matter at first hand.

– There is more now, I ventured, than in earlier ages.

– Indeed, he said, and we owe this good fortune to what? To nothing other than the bigotry and fanaticism of Oliver Cromwell, who, upon being told that the millennium would not arrive till the conversion of the Jews, and on finding that there were none in the kingdom to be converted, promptly insisted that they be invited back for that very purpose.

I was silent.

– Some might say, he ventured, that God works in mysterious ways.

– Memory, he then said, is what separates us from the beasts. How wise then of your people to place memory at the centre of their faith.

– There is, I ventured, such a thing as too much memory. To cling wilfully to memory can lead to the inability to adapt to what is new and changing.

– True, he said, yet of too much memory we can recover, but of none at all?

– We philosophers, he then said, tend to act as though memory did not exist, as though man only consisted of what he saw and felt at a particular moment rather than the sum of what time had done to him.

He was silent again for a long time. The house around us was quite still. The heavy curtains on the windows kept out the least hint of light. I heard him sigh, deep in the recesses of the bed.

– My friend, he said finally, everything you need is provided for you. Should you require anything else you have only to ring. You will come back here tomorrow evening and read to me from a work of your own devising.

– Sir? I said.

– You will read until you hear the first birds of dawn, or till my snores are such as to make it quite certain that I am asleep. Is that understood?

I said that it was.

He was silent again. Then he said:

– It is the silence I cannot bear. When the birds start to sing I know there is a world out there and sleep at once opens its arms to receive me.

I would have suggested to him that overmuch coffee might have rather more to do with his insomnia than any metaphysical doubts concerning the existence of the world, and that a bed less bounded by canopies and curtains might also help him breathe more easily and so bring him on the road towards sleep, but I did not feel it was my place. Besides, we need the fee he is offering if we are to pay for the physician and the roofer.

– Soon they will begin, he said. Soon the air will be full of the sounds of birds.

He was silent then for such a long time that I finally ventured to ask him:

– Do you wish me to go now sir?

– No, he said. Stay till we may hear them.

I waited again for him to speak and he eventually said:

– Are you fond of your little ones?

– Indeed, I said to him. Most fond.

– I have two sons, he said. One of them is an idiot and the other a fool.

I was silent, not knowing how to respond to this.

– Their mother was a fool, he added.

I did not know how to interpret his tone, so kept my peace.

– Fortunately, he said, I have the means to keep them from my presence. For the sight of the one fills me with despair and that of the other with alarm.

He was silent for such a time now that I thought he had verily gone to sleep, but finally he said to me:

– Describe, if you will, the method whereby you compose.

– Sir, I said, I am ever at your service, but you must allow me to retain the secrets of my profession.

– I feared you would say that, he said. Will you not tell me about the methods you employ then?

– I must beg you sir, I said, to leave off such questionings.

– I understand, he said, but there was disappointment in his voice. You may go now.

The lamp was still burning in the drawing-room. I went to the window and drew aside the curtains. A faint glimmer of light rendered visible the lawns, with a thin film of mist lying atop them, and in the distance loomed the great trees of the park, indistinct grey shapes, like nothing so much as chairs and tables when they are covered over to protect them from dust and decay when the owner has closed up the house.

I thought that if the curtains in the corridors were not drawn I would be able to find my way to my room. And indeed they were not, and a few minutes later I was in my bedroom, and had thrown off my clothes and fallen on the bed to sleep through the remaining hours of the night.

The less said about the following day the better. I sat at the elegant desk with the paper and pens within my reach. Again and again I started to write, but nothing came of such beginnings. I pushed back the chair and walked up and down before sitting down again and once more picking up the pen. The result was the same. I took myself into the grounds of the manor and walked, my hands clasped behind my back, my notebook in my pocket, waiting for that little nudge from the gods which would set me going, but, alas, it did not come.

You can imagine that my appetite was not of the best. A most delicious breakfast was served at ten, and an equally good dinner at five, with a simple luncheon in between, but in my anxiety I could do little more than nibble. Oh how I wish you had been there! You would have eaten for the two of us. For my one thought throughout the day was that if I could not satisfy Mr Westfield that evening he would as likely as not send me packing the next day, as he had sent the musician packing before me, and then we would once again have to ask the physician to be patient and the roofer to wait a while before beginning the repairs. And the thought of all these things, which should have acted as a spur to my invention, worked on me instead in the opposite way, and I had, by nightfall, not only not succeeded in finishing anything, I had not even been able to make a start.

After supper I sat at the desk and wrote. Alas, I no longer even tried to fulfil my obligations to my employer, but instead I wrote to you.

I knew of course what he would say. He would call me in and sit me again by his bed, as he had on the previous night.

– Well, my friend, he would say, why do you sit there in silence when you are acquainted with my wishes?

– Alas sir, I would say, you asked me to read from a new composition of my own, and I have to confess that I have none.

– But you knew my wishes, my friend, when you left me last night?

– Indeed I did, sir.

– Are you a writer, my friend?

– I am, sir.

– Then why have you not written?

– One single day, sir, to prepare for a whole night's reading, appears to have been beyond my powers.

– You have enough then for half the night?

– No sir.

– For a quarter then?

– No sir.

– For an hour perhaps?

– Alas, sir, no.

– For half that time?

– No.

– How can you explain this state of affairs, my friend?

– It is not a question, sir, I would say, of beginning at the top left-hand corner, as with the painting of a wall, and then proceeding till the bottom right-hand corner is reached and all is done. It is rather the finding of what I call the thread. With that found, the composition can unwind. But the finding of it is not easy, nor can a set portion of time be allotted to it. It happens sometimes almost at once. At other times many days pass and there is nothing to show for them.

– Mr Goldberg, you were recommended to me as a man in a thousand, as a highly original as well as a thoroughly professional man of letters. Are you telling me that neither you nor your colleagues could fulfil the simple commission I offered you?

– I cannot speak for my colleagues, sir. I can speak only for
myself.

– Speak then, my friend, and defend yourself.

– It may be the case, sir, that in the time of Greece and Rome,
and even in the time of our glorious Shakespeare, a man of letters
might have fulfilled your commission. The writers of those times
might in a day have produced for you a dazzling series of variations on any theme of your choice. You would have had but to
speak, but to outline, however briefly, the subject about which
you wished them to discourse, and in an hour or two, or perhaps
even less, they would have regaled you with the most delightful
fancies and stirring sequences based upon your subject. But, alas,
our own age is grown altogether less inventive and more melan-
cholic, and few can now find it in their hearts 'to take a point at
pleasure and wrest and turn it as he list, making either much or
little of it, according as shall seem best in his own conceit', as an
ancient writer on these matters puts it. For what we list has grown
obscure and difficult to define.

– That is all very well, Mr Goldberg, but you accepted my
commission. Is it not unprofessional of you not to stick to your
word?

– I did not say, sir, that I had been unable to stick to my word.

– You did not? I thought I heard you say most clearly, Mr
Goldberg, that you had.

– May I explain, sir?

– Mr Goldberg, you had better.

– I cannot, as I said, speak for my colleagues, sir, but only for
myself. I have inevitably found that when I am at a loss for a
subject, when the elusive thread of which I was speaking remains
resolutely hidden from sight, then there is one way in which I can
perhaps call it into being.

– And that way, Mr Goldberg?

– That way is to cease to search for themes or for subjects and
to start from the actual position in which I find myself. If that
happens to be a labyrinth from which there seems to be no exit,
that will become my theme. If it is the frustrating search for a
subject which refuses to emerge, then that will be my theme. Do
I make myself clear, sir?

– Go on, Mr Goldberg.

– In the present case I sat down after sampling the delights of the supper with which you had so generously provided me, with my mind made up. I would write the composition for which you asked in the form of a letter to my wife. Not any letter, you understand, sir, but a letter telling her of my visit here and of the circumstances in which I now find myself. In that way, if I do not cover myself with the glory that would accrue to the greatest writers of the past, I at least do not cover myself with shame, and I fulfil, in my own way, the commission you have given me.

– In the letter, then, I tell my wife of my arrival at your house, of my first meeting with you, and of the first night, in which you so generously consented to share your thoughts with a mere scribbler like myself. I tell her about your instructions to me, and about my inability to carry them out, and my final, albeit grossly inadequate, solution to the problem. It is not, as I say, the most elegant solution in the world, and I would, I assure you, have produced a more elegant had I been able. But we, today, can only do what we can, not what we would, and this was a solution of sorts, not perhaps entirely without its own kind of elegance. May it at least have the desired effect.

2. Westfield

Mr Tobias Westfield of Somerton Hall in the county of B—— had not always suffered from insomnia. Lying awake, night after night, in the pitch darkness, ensconced in the large four-poster bed he had inherited from his parents, James and Eliza Westfield, he tried in vain to remember when it was he had first found it difficult to sleep. As on all previous nights, his search ended in failure. He turned, first on his right side and then on his left; he lay on his stomach and then on his back; he punched the pillows and doubled them over so as to raise his head well above the level of his body, or threw them to the foot of the bed and lay quite flat. But sleep would not come to him, nor the answer to his question.

He had tried counting sheep leaping over a fence, horses fording a river and frogs hopping from lily-pad to lily-pad; he had tried to think of all the poets whose names began with S and of all the painters whose names began with M; he had endeavoured to recall Plato's proof of the immortality of the soul and Anselm's of the existence of God. But just as he was drifting off to sleep on the backs of the sheep or the wings of the Ideas, there would pop into his head, out of nowhere, the image of himself in his four-poster bed in the darkened room in Somerton Hall, surrounded by its great park, and at once he would be wide awake and knowing that he would have to go through the whole dreary ritual once again.

He was, by nature, a cheerful soul, but these bouts of insomnia affected him profoundly. He did not exactly cease to be cheerful, but he now often caught himself being cheerful. In the midst of his cheer the thought would suddenly cross his mind: what a cheerful fellow I am at heart, in spite of everything – and at once gloom would settle on his spirits.

Never for long, of course. He would shake his head to clear it and resume his current occupation. He went on being the happy, compassionate and charming companion his friends had always known. But it began to prey on his mind, this feeling that nothing could now happen unrecorded, so to speak. Moreover, the one thing he could not do was will himself to sleep, though his physician, Dr Carpenter, and James Ballantyne, his friend and neighbour, both insisted such a thing was possible.

– Tell yourself that you are not going to fret any more, Ballantyne would say. Compose yourself in the most comfortable position. If you feel inclined to move, resist it for as long as possible. Only if the need becomes imperative, succumb to it. For then it would clearly be much worse to resist.

– But how am I to know when it becomes imperative? Westfield asked him. How do I know it is not merely a weakening of the will?

– These things are obvious, Ballantyne would say gruffly, for all the world as though his friend were determined to be difficult.

But the problem was that they had ceased to be obvious to Westfield. He now no longer knew whether he was being weak or strong, indulgent or stoical, abject or heroic.

Dr Carpenter recommended a trip abroad, and assured him that by the time he returned he would not even remember the anxieties that had once afflicted him. He went into France, and then into Italy, returning by way of the Rhine and the Low Countries. He did not tell his doctor of the agonies he had suffered on the road, unable to decide whether to stop at some charming spot for two nights or three, unable to make up his mind whether to travel straight from one major city to the next, and thus leave himself more time to enjoy the famous sights, or to go slowly and explore at least some of the many fascinating byways of the route. And always, of course, unable to sleep.

It is true that most nights he did drop off, exhausted, for an hour or two. But going to sleep in the first place was agony and it was even worse when he woke up in the middle of the night in an alien bed and room. Then he would gaze out into the darkness, trying to discern the outline of the window and the shape of the cupboard against the further wall, only to discover that he had in fact been staring straight at the wall against which his bed stood. Panic would then seize him and he would fumble for the matches and feel for his candle and only breathe freely again when, in the flickering light of the candle, the actual contours of the room and its furnishings were revealed to him. On many nights he did not sleep at all.

Nature, though, had always been a great solace to him. He had spent many hours in the extensive park of Somerton Hall in the days following his father's untimely death (his mother's, when he was only nine, he could not remember making any impression on him), and had been soothed by his walks along the edge of the lake and through the woods. But in the course of one of his sleepless nights, somewhere between Basle and Cologne, the phrase suddenly came unbidden into his mind: *Nature, though, had always been a great solace to him*. After that it was as though some spell had been broken. His head would lift as he stepped out into the woods on a bright summer morning, and he would laugh aloud for sheer joy, and then at once the image of himself laughing and the sound of the words *his heart would lift as he stepped out* would fill his head and drive the happiness from his heart and the laughter from his throat.

The way he put it to himself was that everything had developed an echo. And just as a continuous echo destroys the initial sound, so it was with his life. Everything he did, everything he thought, everything he saw, now carried its echo within it. He knew in advance, even as he prepared to rejoice over something, that his happiness would soon be clouded by the thought that what he was experiencing now he had experienced before and would no doubt experience again. Nothing was simply itself any more, it was always one of a series, stretching backwards and forwards into infinity. If he took a step he was aware of the fact that he had taken countless such steps before and would, no doubt, by the time of his death, have taken countless more; if he read a book he had the feeling that he had done this so often in the past that it was only habit that kept him at it. Even the voices and gestures of his friends and of those in attendance on him began to seem like mere echoes of their natural voices and gestures, switched on by some hidden mechanism and to be switched off again as soon as they had left his presence.

He began to get the feeling that it was up to him to hold the world together. This was a task that required his utmost concentration and all his will-power at every moment of the day and night. If he relaxed for even an instant the world threatened to fly apart into a myriad fragments or else simply to fizzle out. So now it was no longer only a matter of being unable to sleep; it was rather that he had a duty to remain wakeful, for if he inadvertently nodded off he sensed that some calamity far beyond his worst imaginings would overtake not just himself but the entire universe. Sometimes, indeed, he did doze off, but such lapses must have passed unnoticed because although he started up from these states with a cold horror clutching at his heart, nothing round him seemed to have changed.

And food, he found, had lost its taste, or else he had lost the taste for it. He would stare at his plate for minutes on end, move some of the items around on it with his fork, then lay down the fork with a sigh and push the plate from him. He grew thinner and thinner and his eyes grew bigger and bigger as his face wasted away. – You look almost distinguished, his friend Ballantyne joked, but secretly he confessed to Dr Carpenter:

– Something must be done for the man. He cannot go on in this way much longer.

– What would you suggest? asked Dr Carpenter.

– You're the doctor, not me, Ballantyne replied.

– I have never met a case like it, Dr Carpenter confessed. Though I did once hear of one in Bohemia.

The body, however, normally has an answer in such instances. Westfield, at this point, developed a fever and was confined to his bed. It was said later that he had to be chained to it, for he would leap up and attack those who ministered to him; and even that he had been gagged, since he had taken to howling like a dog or wolf and the servants felt themselves being driven mad by the inhuman sounds. He, however, always denied such stories, saying that he had been an exemplary patient, that the fever had so exhausted him that he lay helpless in the great bed for so long that all around him had despaired of his recovery. But then, as if he had had to reach the point almost of non-existence before the spirit which tormented him consented to leave his body, he began to recover. His fever dropped as abruptly as it had arisen, and one day, taking his midday broth, he felt the golden taste of chicken on his palate and his heart leaped as it had not done for many a day.

Having recovered, and finding that his insomnia showed no sign of returning, he decided to get married, and, his choice having fallen on the nineteen-year-old daughter of one of his mother's oldest friends, and she having accepted him, they celebrated their wedding in style and then travelled to Venice for their honeymoon. Shortly after their return, though, his young wife began to complain of a pain in her chest and within three months she had wasted away and died.

These things happen, and Westfield accepted it with resignation. The memory of his wife's youthful laughter would return to haunt him throughout his subsequent life, bringing with it always a little pang of pain at having enjoyed her company for so short a time, but otherwise he no longer thought of her. Having married once it was only natural that he should think of doing so again. His second wife, people said, was even prettier than the first, and had the additional advantage of being distantly related to him, for she was the daughter of a second cousin of his father, and he had once spent a whole summer with her, in the far-off days of his earliest childhood. Unfortunately she had developed into a brainless chatterbox, the kind of woman, his friend Ballantyne would say, on whom one would like to be able to bring down the lid.

Westfield fathered two children upon her, then ceased to sleep with her or even to see her. He made provisions for the bringing up of his children, and for his wife's well-being, but himself retired to a single wing of Somerton Hall, where, shutting himself up in his father's library for large portions of the day, he read his way through the volumes his father and grandfather had accumulated. Despite his reclusive life, however, he still saw his old friends and retained his innate cheerfulness of manner. The death of his second wife, killed by a fall from the horse she had taken to riding at a furious gallop over ditch and dale in the early hours of each morning, out of bitterness, it was said, at the way her husband had treated her and her sorrow at the fact that one of her children had turned out to be subnormal – her death caused even less of a ripple than had that of his first wife. At least, he confessed to his friend Ballantyne, marriage to her has cured me once and for all of any desire for the state of matrimony.

She was buried next to the first Mrs Westfield in the family vault. Provision having already been made for the care of his younger and the education of his elder boy, he himself went on living in the west wing of the manor, reading, entertaining his friends and neighbours, and occasionally travelling abroad to meet some of the many distinguished scientists and men of letters with whom he had taken to corresponding.

From an interest in Roman law, which he had developed in his twenties, he had turned to the study of Sanskrit, then to the architecture of the pyramids, and finally to the thought systems of mankind. He held the view that there were, basically, only seven original ideas dreamed up by the human race, each of which had been endlessly recycled, adorned, slimmed down, blown up, or stood upon its head. He had often thought of committing his theories to paper, but laziness and a keen sense of what would be lost in suppleness thereby always held him back. He did occasionally scribble down little diagrams and tables, or roughly sketch in the genealogies of one or other of the seven ideas, but these he quickly scratched out or tore up, as though their presence in the world robbed them of the life and resonance he felt them to have so long as they remained in his head.

One night, several years after the death of his second wife, he woke up when everything was still dark and silent all around him, and found he could not go back to sleep. He lay prone in the middle of the large four-poster bed he had inherited from his parents and thought about immortality. It seemed to him entirely natural that once men came to consciousness they should desire some reassurance that they would not simply vanish without a trace when their life was done. He had studied the religious systems of the world and found that they all testified to this truth, that men do not like to think that that which is doing the thinking will in the not very distant future not be doing it any more. He had come to the conclusion that though there is no personal immortality we do in a sense live on in the memories of others. Such an after-life, he thought, is by no means infinite, and it should be possible by means of fairly simple calculations, to plot the gradual fading of the memory of a dead person, as first those who had known them passed away, and then those who had known the knowers and then those who had known those who had known the knowers. He worked out tentatively that forty-three years and four months was the average period of survival, at least in the countries of the civilised world, as memory gave way to hearsay and hearsay to rumour and rumour itself eventually died away. In the case of men or women of renown, of course, the matter was a little more complicated. Memories of their exploits, if they had been soldiers or statesmen, would of course never wholly die out, though in a relatively short space of time it would become extremely difficult to disentangle legend from truth, as had happened, for example, in the cases of Alexander, Arthur and Richard III. Where artists were concerned matters were even harder to determine, for in one sense they could be said to live on in their works so long as these were read or looked at, but then in exactly what sense could they be said to live on in this way?

Since his youthful bouts of insomnia, leading to his illness and temporary insanity, Westfield had not been in the habit of waking up in the middle of the night, and even less of finding that half an hour after such an occurrence he had still not gone back to sleep. For many years now he had been able to contemplate his early illness with equanimity, as though it had happened to someone else, but now a tiny seed of doubt was planted in his mind. Did such things recur? Was he still in some essential way the same person as the youthful idealist who had walked the grounds of Somerton Hall at dawn, listening to the birds, and spent a joyous fortnight in Venice with his youthful bride? He tried lying on his back with his eyes closed, then on his stomach, and finally on his right side and then on his left. Eventually he rolled over once more onto his back, but this time with his eyes wide open, staring out into the darkness above.

He had forgotten that time could pass so slowly. He kept listening out for signs of his household coming to life, but there was not a sound to be heard.

this time, he thought to himself. I will
ht away.

d seemed during the night as though
vn – he summoned his physician. But
mbling that nature should be allowed
y recommend a trip abroad. Westfield
happened the last time he had tried
old physician suggested he try taking
nnounced that he had no intentions
itual abode.

w up his hands and said that so long
nd he had no reason to doubt that at
l do nothing. Westfield thereupon
the matter due thought he asked that
d a harpsichord installed in the room
man was hired to play throughout the
tening to the instrument, Westfield
soothing arms of Morpheus.

er, proved sadly mistaken. He had
c and found the constant twanging of
is nerves even more than the silence
ugh, he said to the man, shortly after
ht. Collect your wages in the morning

ndeed doomed to stay awake twenty-
ld make the most if it, and asked for
a light to be placed beside his bed and the curtains of the bed
drawn back. He would read the whole night through, and perhaps
take a walk in the park in the early hours of the morning.

But when the time came he found that his eyes would not
remain open, though his mind unfortunately raced as fast as ever,
He kept yawning compulsively, even though sleep continued to
evade him. The memory of the previous periods of insomnia
came back to him, and his heart missed a beat as he recalled all
that had gone with it. Stop! he said to himself, I am not a child any
longer. If I can never be a fully normal human being let me at least
adjust like an adult to my condition.

With that peace came to him and he slept. And for a week afterwards, apart from a short period of anxiety when he first crept between the sheets, the curse seemed to have been lifted from him and he would fall asleep and not wake up till his manservant entered the room in the morning with his tea and drew back the curtains.

But his hopes were short-lived. The brief preliminary period of anxiety grew longer and longer, and soon he was lucky if he was able to snatch an hour or two of fitful sleep in the course of the whole night.

He now tried to repress the fear that he knew lay in wait to engulf him as soon as he put his head on his pillow. Tomorrow, he thought, I will make enquiries about hiring someone to read to me.

And with that thought he fell asleep.

3. Maria

What she loved most of all was listening to her father read to her from Mr Pope's Homer. And the bit of Homer she loved most of all was when twinkle-toed Thetis, the daughter of the old man of the sea and the mother of Achilles, goes up to Olympus to visit the bandy-legged smith Hephaestos, to ask him a great favour. Hector has stripped Achilles' armour off his dear friend Patroclus after he has killed him, the armour Achilles had lent him to protect him in battle. Now Achilles has vowed revenge; but how is he to go into battle without armour? Twinkle-toed Thetis pays a call on Hephaestos and his charming wife Charis. You? the surprised Charis says. To what do we owe the honour of this call when you never ever come to visit us? She asks her in and makes her welcome while she calls out to her husband: Look who's here, darling! Bandy-legs comes to the door of his workshop, sees who it is and exclaims: Thetis! My dear! What wouldn't I do for the one who saved my life? So he goes back in, tidies up carefully, puts away his anvil and bellows, for a good craftsman always looks after his tools, wipes himself down, washes the grime and sweat from his pores and puts on a clean shirt and tie. Then, supported by his delightful automated maidens, cunningly devised and constructed by himself to make light of his deformity, he enters the drawing-room. Meanwhile, Charis has sat the visitor down on a comfortable chair with a footstool to match and gone off to see what delicacies there are in the house for the unexpected guest.

Maria could never have enough of this passage, when she grew up she wanted to be like Thetis, firm and resourceful, determined to help her son in his hour of need, though always full of sorrow and anxiety at having a mortal for a child. Meanwhile her father went on reading Homer to her and she slowly grew up. So loving was her father, so full of tender care, that she hardly missed the mother she had never known. At eighteen she was ready for marriage and there, asking for her hand, was the handsome Mr Westfield. But if all he had been was handsome, and an older man, she would have been wary. What drew her to him was his ability to tell jokes and the way his eyes puckered at the corners when he laughed as he talked to her father, a cup of tea in his hand.

She had known from the day he first came to the house that sooner or later he would propose, but when the time came it was still a shock, pleasurable, but a shock nonetheless. Do you think I should, Papa? she asked. You must do whatever you think is right, my dear, her father said. I would not want to abandon you, Papa, she said. My dear, he said, I shall not feel abandoned thinking of you living nearby, happy and safe.

Even so, she felt a twinge of pain as he led her up the aisle and gave her away to her future husband. But they had talked much about this moment, in the weeks before the ceremony, and he had pointed out to her that, were she not to marry and have children of her own, were she to remain with him forever and devote her life to him, the years could only sour their relationship; whereas now they could move forward as they needed to and as God required. He spoke with eminent good sense, as he had always done, ever since she could remember. But, despite all this, she felt that moment as a kind of death.

Yet Westfield, if he had not the stature of Achilles, was much the handsomest man she had ever seen, and kind and witty as well. He was taking her to Venice for their honeymoon and the excitement of the journey helped calm her pain.

In Venice he had taken an apartment in a splendid palazzo, looking out on to one of the quieter canals. A boy took their trunks out of the gondola and, with no apparent sign of effort, carried them up to their rooms. She ran to the window and threw back the shutters. Unfortunately the skies, which had been so blue on their arrival, had grown overcast, and as she put her arm out of the window in a gesture she herself did not understand, she felt on her open palm the first small drops of rain.

Her husband was in the other room, but the boy was standing by the trunks, apparently waiting for something. That will be all, she said, thank you. She saw then that he was hardly a boy, not even a very young man, more a person of her own age or even a little older. Thank you, she said again. He looked at her with eyes, she now saw, like the dark lagoon itself, but did not move. Then, very slowly, the skin of one eyelid came down over the eye.

She turned back to the window, waiting for him to leave. Then she heard her husband in the room, turned round again and found the man had gone.

– He was waiting for something, she said. Perhaps he was waiting to be paid.

– Who? asked Westfield, who had come close to her at the window and taken her in his arms.

– The boy who brought the luggage.

He didn't answer.

– Didn't you see him? she said. He was waiting for something.

– No, he said, holding her close. There was nobody there. He had already been paid.

The journey had been a tiring one, but they were both young and strong and soon recovered. The skies cleared and they set out to explore the city.

Westfield, it turned out, had many friends in Venice, who did their best to make their stay there as pleasant and rich in culture as possible.

One evening, though, she decided she would prefer to stay at home and let her husband go out alone. She sat by the window and looked out at the canal, wondering how her father was, at home in England, and thinking of all she would have to tell him on her return.

Gradually she became aware of a figure standing on the narrow path on the other side of the canal, looking up at her. It was the boy, or man, who had carried up their luggage. He was staring straight at her window and she, suddenly meeting his gaze, waved at him, anxious to make up for any bad impression he might have had of her that day. But he merely went on gazing at her and did not respond.

Embarrassed, she left the window and went to sit inside the

room. But she could not concentrate on the book she had picked up and got up a little while later and approached the window again, careful this time not to let herself be seen. Slowly she moved her head until she could see across the canal, but everything, as usual, was deserted.

That night she dreamed of the boy. Her husband lay asleep beside her and she dreamed that Hephaestos was handing her the great shield he had just made for her son. On it the whole earth was depicted, and the sun and the moon and all the stars. He showed her the earth, and her father standing in his orchard, lost in thought, and then he showed her the view from her window in the palazzo in Venice, and there, on the other side of the canal, was the boy. This time, though, as she gazed at him, the eyelid slowly came down over his eye while the rest of his face remained expressionless. She lay asleep in the Venetian heat next to her husband and in her dream Hephaestos was telling her about the shield he had wrought for her son. His thick finger moved over the shield and pointed at seas and islands and mountains and great forests. He showed her oxen ploughing fields, turning the rich earth, and, elsewhere, two men fighting in the midst of a group of screaming spectators. She was fascinated by the thick finger as it moved on remorselessly over the giant shield, stabbing at this spot or that, while the deep voice rolled over her. Then she realised that the deep voice was that of her husband, asking her if she would like some breakfast.

The days flew by in a whirl of activity: they visited churches and took a boat out to the islands, they dined with their friends and went to the opera. On the last day of their stay an outing had been planned to the furthest island of the lagoon, but when she woke up that day she knew what she wanted:

– I want to be by myself, she said. He asked her if she was not feeling well, but she assured him that she was, that she only needed to have a day to herself before the long journey home.

She waited with impatience for him to leave, but when he had gone and the house had fallen silent she began to feel restless. She went to the window and looked out at the gloomy canal below. She sat there for a long time, but no boat passed and the bank opposite remained deserted. Finally she got out her bonnet and cape and decided to go for a walk. She did not know what she was looking for, but she felt that it was something important.

Outside it had begun to drizzle, though the air was warm. She walked quickly, looking straight ahead of her, turning corners and crossing bridges at random. The drizzle had turned into a steady rain, and she knew it would be wiser to go back. But this was the first time she had been on her own in the city and she felt it was up to her to make the most of it. It was as if she would not grow up if she did not find what she was seeking, though that she was seeking anything at all was more than she would have acknowledged, even to herself.

She had come to a part of the town which she did not know and could not remember ever visiting. The streets were wider, the houses more dilapidated than elsewhere, and every now and again she would catch a glimpse of the sea, between the houses. She realised suddenly that she was wet through and through. At once she felt utterly miserable. The pleasant sense of adventure with which she had set out had completely disappeared and now she was only cold and wet and very tired.

She tried to retrace her steps, but all the streets looked the same and she could not tell, when she came to a particular bridge or square, if she had been there before or not. The rain had begun to penetrate her clothing and to trickle down her bare skin, and she shivered and had to clamp her jaws together to prevent her teeth from chattering. She started to ask the way but the people she met only shrugged their shoulders and walked on. Though she kept telling herself that she could not get lost, that Venice was small enough and she had the address firmly in her head, she could not prevent herself from panicking. Now she was running up one alley and back, going over a bridge and then deciding that she would return on the other side. The skies were black and a wind had arisen, sweeping the heavy rain into her face whichever way she turned.

At once she emerged into the square of St Mark's. There was the cathedral in front of her, and she realised with a burst of indignation at herself that of course she should have been asking for directions to St Mark's all along, for there was no mistaking the route from there to their palazzo.

Inside the house everything was quiet, though she could hardly believe that they could be picnicking in this weather. She took off her wet clothes and found that she could not stop her teeth from chattering. She had thought of putting on dry clothes but instead pulled on her nightgown and crept into bed.

So it was that on her return to England she was riven by a hacking cough and a low fever which would not leave her, and, despite everything the doctors could do, went into a decline. Her father came and sat by her bed, but she was too weak even to ask him to read to her. She wanted to tell him about the boy who had winked at her, but forebore. He held her hand and she recalled the sorrow of Thetis the silver-footed one at the thought that she had married a mortal and that her son was doomed to die. That is why, as she felt her end approaching, she pressed her father's hand ever more strongly, as though to convey to him her understanding of the fact that the one who remains inevitably suffers more than the one who passes away.

4. In the Carriage (1)

– I was reading the other day, Hammond says as the carriage rolls along, about this wild boy they have found in the forests of South West France. Has this come to your attention, Mr Goldberg?

    – Indeed it has, Goldberg says.

    – And what is your opinion on the subject? asks Hammond.

    – Of the boy himself or of the speculations surrounding him?

    – Both, Hammond says. Both.

    – There is a wild boy in us all, is there not? says Goldberg. It does not take much to let him out.

    – True, Hammond says. True.

    – It does not take much, Goldberg says, to reduce us to his level.

    – Then you do not hold with the theories of M. Rousseau, Hammond says, that it is to his exalted level that we should all aspire?

    – M. Rousseau and his opponents all speak the same language, Goldberg says. For the one our present civilisation shows us the depths to which man can fall, for the others the heights to which he can rise. What is there to choose between them?

    – As far as this boy is concerned, Hammond asks, do you incline to the theory that he belongs to the species of wild wolf children, or that he is merely an idiot, or that he is an imposter who will sooner or later be unmasked?

    – The latter hypothesis has little to recommend it, Goldberg says. For what advantage would there be for an imposter in suffering humiliation and imprisonment without any compensatory benefits?

– Would you say then, Hammond presses him, that he is one of the species of wild boy or merely a poor idiot?

– Consider the facts, Mr Hammond, Goldberg says. The boy was first sighted, I believe, several years ago in the forests of the Tarn. Then, a few months later, a group of hunters came upon him in a clearing and pounced upon him. Though he struggled they held him fast, but, when he seemed docile at last and they were leading him back to their village with the minimum of constraint, he once more contrived to escape. Yet a few weeks later he knocked of his own accord on the door of an outlying house, followed the housewife inside when she opened to him, and settled on the floor by the fire at her feet. He seemed unable to speak or to hear when spoken to, and unwilling to eat anything save the raw potatoes which he himself threw into the fire and plucked out as they burned, at no small harm to himself. Again, though, before he could be taken away and examined by a physician he had made good his escape, and it was only several months later that he was finally caught for good and detained under careful supervision in the district, before being transported to Paris for proper examination by the authorities.

– At this point, Goldberg says, it seems that he was handed over to the inspector of the asylum for the deaf, a certain M. Itard, on order from the Minister of the Interior, for him to investigate the boy's condition thoroughly and draw up a report on it. M. Itard has now reported on the results of these six months of intensive observation. What conclusion has he reached?

– You agree then with the diagnosis of M. Itard? Hammond asks. That the boy is no idiot but will in time and with sufficient care being devoted to his education, become a worthwhile citizen?

– I did not say that, Goldberg answers.

– What then? Hammond asks. You reject his diagnosis?

– I did not say that either, Goldberg says.

– Proceed, Mr Goldberg, proceed, Hammond says. Forgive my interruptions.

– It seems, Goldberg says, that M. Itard has established that though the boy is dumb there is no physical malformation which would render him incapable of human speech. And though he seems deaf to the most violent noises, such as a musket fired at close quarters, his hearing is most acute when it concerns something he conceives to be of interest to him, such as the opening of a door behind him, which might allow him to make a dash for freedom, or even when a nut is cracked on the other side of the room, since he is extremely partial to nuts. He will often smile and greet M. Itard when the latter enters his room, but he is just as often withdrawn and indifferent, quite unresponsive even to the most friendly overtures. And there are times too when he will kick and bite those who come close to him, or beat his head against a wall in a paroxysm of rage and anger. What are we to make of these shards of conflicting evidence?

– What indeed? Hammond says. M. Itard presents us with a creature who appears to flout all the rules of normal behaviour.

– What I have found most interesting, Goldberg says, is what M. Itard has let us see about the boy's relation to language. For all are agreed that if the boy could use language either to speak or to write, he would quickly adapt himself to the ways of civilisation.

– M. Itard certainly has high hopes of his progress in this area, Hammond says. It seems that in a few months the boy has already made sufficient progress to be able to recognise words and to relate them to the objects they designate. Surely it is only a matter of time before he acquires a sufficient store of such words to enable him to converse with his keeper?

– Is it? Mr Hammond, Goldberg says. I grant you that that is the conclusion M. Itard would draw from his experiments, but I wonder if it is the right conclusion.

– Surely, Hammond says, and at that moment the carriage hits a stone and the two are hurled into each other's arms. When they have disentangled themselves and straightened their clothing, Hammond resumes.

– Surely, he says, if in these few months, when we must take into account the anxieties and confusions likely to beset one who has had his tenor of life radically altered, the boy has been able to relate an already sizeable number of words to the objects they designate, there is no reason why he should not in the fullness of time acquire a sufficient vocabulary to enable him to join the ranks of ordinary men and women?

– That, says Goldberg, is where I strongly disagree. Consider the evidence. M. Itard has filled in six cards, writing upon each in large letters the names of the objects on which he has placed the cards, viz. BOOK, BOX, DISH, HAMMER, etc. He removes the objects and takes them into an adjoining room. Then he returns. The boy is sitting at the table with the inscribed cards before him. M. Itard picks up the card marked BOOK and hands it to him. The boy takes it and goes into the next room. He returns with the book, which had previously rested under the card, and which he has found on the table in the next room.

– Which suggests, Hammond intrudes, that he can carry the idea of a book in his head, for a limited period at least.

– The period is immaterial, says Goldberg. For me the most significant aspect of the whole project is this: that if the precise book once laid beneath the card is missing from the other room the boy returns crestfallen after a lengthy search. It never seems to enter his head that he could have brought *another* book from the room, which, we must presume, houses a considerable number of them.

– But that will surely come in time, Hammond says.

– I wonder, Goldberg says. For consider. To grasp that the specific book first laid under the card and now openly displayed on the table in the library, or perhaps now hidden by M. Itard, is but an example of the species *book*, requires an understanding of what a book is, what it is used for in our society. Books are not objects so many inches across by so many inches down by so many inches in thickness. They can be any size and, indeed, any shape, so long as they consist of pages of writing bound together between covers. But unless you already form part of a society which uses books, which reads them or has seen others reading them and knows what it is they are doing, how will you make the transition from this particular book to any book? To move from the book as object, from *this* book as *this* object, to the notion of the book in general, just as to move from *this* box or dish or hammer to the generality of boxes or dishes or hammers, requires a sense of *how* these objects are used. This the child normally discovers in the course of his first years, just as he discovers everything about the way society functions and learns in time to use

the objects of society for himself, by reading or eating off plates
or putting things in boxes or hammering in a nail. But can this be
imparted to one who is already past his tenth year? To one who
has had no benefit of civil society and is himself not in any way
involved in it?

– But surely, Hammond says, given time –

– I do not think time is the essence of the problem, Goldberg
says. Though I wish M. Itard well in his efforts, I fear that the
remarkable early advances his devotion to the boy has produced
will not be continued, and soon he and all the world will lose
interest in poor Victor, as they have chosen to call him, and leave
him to rot in some miserable hole.

– You are too pessimistic, Mr Goldberg, Hammond says.

– I am well aware of the fragility of what we call civilisation,
Goldberg says. I am well aware of how little it would take to turn
you or me into Victors and how little even the most well-meaning
would be able to do for us then. It takes years for us to feel our
way into society, years in which, with luck, our parents will help
and protect us, but it takes very little to throw us back into the
darkness.

– What would, in your opinion, Mr Goldberg, constitute that
little?

– I am not much past my fiftieth year, Goldberg says, and my
health, thank God, is robust enough. Yet these days I often find
myself struggling to recall the name of an object of daily use to
which I find myself needing to refer, such as a knife or a lemon. I
can see the object in my mind's eye, and I know that all my
conscious life I have had no trouble finding its name. But now I
have to pause and try to recollect: It is not a fork, it is not a spoon,
it is that other thing, ah yes, it is a knife. It is not an orange, it is
not an apple, it is not a pear, it is that sour and greenish yellow
fruit, it is, it is – ah yes, it is a lemon. When such lapses occur,
Goldberg says, and they occur more and more frequently these
days, I have the sense that the whole skein of wool could very
quickly unravel and I would in barely an instant be left speech-
less and bereft.

– Such things have occasionally occurred to me in my dreams,
Hammond says, but not, so far, in real life.

– If you have dreamed about them you will know what I mean, Goldberg says. And why I say that our grip on language and therefore on civil society is fragile in the extreme.

The two are silent.

– I knew a man, Goldberg says, looking out of the window of the carriage at the landscape hurrying past them, who, one day, after thirty years of married life, looked at his toothbrush one evening and no longer knew what it was. He brought it into the bedroom and handed it to his wife. What is this? he asked her. Why, she said, a toothbrush, of course. Toothbrush? he said. The words, he told me, sounded strange to his ears. He turned the object round and continued to examine it. A toothbrush, his wife said again. To brush your teeth with. Ah, he said. He sat on the edge of the bed beside her, holding the toothbrush in his hand and looking at it quizzically. Go on, she said. Put it back where you found it. He did as he was told and returned to bed. By the next morning he had forgotten the entire incident. But later that day, when he went into the bathroom and saw his toothbrush again, it all came back to him. Now he had no trouble relating to it at all. It was his toothbrush and there was an end to it. But, he told me, he could now still vividly recall his puzzlement that evening, his sense of not knowing in the least what a humble object in daily use *was*, or what it was *used for*.

Hammond is silent, his eyes too on the landscape. Finally he says: – Was that man by any chance yourself, Mr Goldberg?

– Perhaps, Goldberg says, we are only fully human when we recognise that there is a wild boy in all of us and that he is where we begin and where no doubt we shall end.

– Come come, Mr Goldberg, Hammond says. I grant you that because the boy is a human being we can extend our sympathy to him, but that does not mean that we should identify with him.

– My conclusion, Goldberg says, is that he is neither a wild boy nor an idiot, because both these terms seek to place him at a distance from us, whereas what he has to teach us, what his sad case has to teach us, Mr Hammond, is that it is only too easy for any of us to slip through the meshes with which we are bound to society and to ourselves.

– Your sophistries make my head swim, Hammond says.

– I am sincerely sorry for it, Goldberg says.

They are silent and, together, gaze out of the window of the carriage.

Goldberg takes his watch out of his pocket and examines it.

– Do not fret, Mr Goldberg, Hammond says. We will soon be there.

Goldberg replaces the watch in his pocket and turns to him, smiling.

5. The Sand

By far the most vivid picture available in Britain of the material equipment and domestic economy of a Neolithic community is to be seen at the celebrated prehistoric village of Skara Brae, overlooking the shore of the beautiful Bay of Skaill on the Western coast of the mainland of Orkney. In the course of ages the sea has carried away a large proportion of the village, but seven huts still remain, forming a cluster, closely huddled together, and connected by a series of winding, roofed-in and crazy-paved alleys, with a small open paved area towards the west end of what may be called, with some exaggeration of language, for it barely exceeds thirty-five metres in length, the main street. All the huts were built of local stone – flagstones, sandstones, indurated shale – and are more or less rectangular. The average dimension is about fifteen feet square. The walls are carefully constructed in horizontal courses, the stones being accurately fitted together but not laid in lime or even in clay. Each hut is entered by a low paved passage through its outer wall, usually from five to eight feet in thickness. Set well back in this passage is a door, probably a slab of stone, but sometimes of whale-bone, let into sockets on either side of the passage. In one hut the stone draw-bar was actually found in position, and in one the sockets were fitted onto the outside, suggesting that it had been used as the local prison. Since no timber appears to have been available to the villagers, it is likely that the span of the roof was completed by whale-bone rafters, obtained from stranded animals, and covered with sods or thatch. On that wind-swept site a tent-like covering of skins would not have survived for long; and in any case the roofs of the entire village had eventually to support a considerable wealth of extraneous material. In the middle of each hut is a hearth, and beside it sometimes an oven. Against the side walls are beds or bunks, skilfully fashioned out of stone slabs. One bed on the right hand side is always larger, and doubtless belonged to the head of the house. At the back of the hut is a stone dresser with two shelves. In the walls are various keeping-places, sometimes shelved. In the floors are sunk little boxes, carefully lined with clay, as if to contain water. It is thought that these may have been used for storage of shell-fish. The entire village was externally buried in its own midden refuse. It is clear that the inhabitants deliberately heaped this stuff over the whole place, leaving a vent above each hut for the peat-smoke to escape. Thus the village must have looked like a giant anthill with crater-like smoke-holes over each dwelling and two or three tunnel-like entries on the flanks. Today the whole is open to the skies and the visitor may wander at will and upright through the whole minuscule settlement.

The inhabitants of Skara Brae had no knowledge of metal, nor of tilling the ground. They were pastoral folk, tending their herds of scraggy, long-horned cattle and flocks of little, tousled, long-legged sheep. The number of young cattle whose remains have been found on the site shows that, as always in ancient times, lack of winter feed necessitated a wholesale slaughter in the autumn. The large proportion of bullocks points to the practice of gelding. For the rest, their diet seems to have consisted of edible shell-fish, though, rather surprisingly, little fishing or seal-hunting seems to have been practised. The Skara Brae folk made themselves pottery, but in this they were not very expert, possibly because for firing they had no other fuel than peat. On the other hand they were good at working stone: their axe-heads and other implements are competently cut, and they showed real mastery in carving highly decorated knobbed or spiked stone balls, the use of which has not been ascertained. Many articles were made of bone or horn, and the villagers appear to have used no imported material of any kind. They did not know how to weave or spin and probably wore skins. For ornament they made themselves necklaces of sheep-bones, teeth of cattle and killer-whales, and walrus or narwhal ivory. Little pots of stone or whale-bone, containing white, blue, red or yellow ochre, permit us to infer that they painted their bodies.

As at Pompeii, the end of Skara Brae came suddenly. The Bay of Skaill is scoured by fierce south-westerly gales; and one wild day a storm of exceptional severity engulfed the village in sand. The inhabitants had to bolt for their lives, leaving all their possessions behind them. 'One woman in her haste to squeeze through the narrow door of her home,' writes the archaeologist V. Gordon Childe, who has done more than anyone to reconstruct for us the way of life of these people, 'broke her necklace and left a string of beads behind as she scampered up the passage.'

For thousands of years the village lay under sand, lost and forgotten. Then one day, in the year 1851, another fierce storm swept the Orkneys and when it had subsided the tiny settlement was again revealed, exactly as it had been when the sand engulfed it.

6. The Fool

My father is a fool. He gives himself airs and stays up all night reading books of metaphysics and philosophy, and prides himself on the fact that he has corresponded with 'the greatest spirits of the age'. You are not to touch that, that is a letter from Mr Gibbon. This is the file of my correspondence with Mr Hume. When M. Voltaire was so good as to seek my advice. The great Goethe himself has deigned to enquire. And so on. Somewhere in the library is to be found the letter he received from none other than God himself. I made sure I was there when he opened it. Strange, he said, scanning it for the signature. Then he put it down and looked at me long and hard. I affected indifference and stared out of the window. He picked it up again and read it through with care. When he came to the passage about in every age there is but one person chosen by me etc., he laid the letter on his lap and closed his eyes. I could see he was troubled. M. Voltaire and Herr Goethe are prize correspondents but God is something else altogether. He turned the envelope this way and that and held it up to the light, perhaps he was looking for an address to which to send a reply. Do you know anything about this? he eventually asked me. What? I said, feigning ignorance. This letter, he said. Who is it from? I asked. He shook his head in frustration and did not reply. I could see his suspicions were aroused, as indeed I knew they would be, but I could see too that his foolish conceit and credulity would win out in the end. What is strange? I asked him, but he only shook his head again and laid the letter in his desk, which he then closed and locked, pocketing the key. He returned to his chair and sat again, pressing the tips of his fingers together and gazing down at them, no doubt waiting for me to leave before composing a reply, though how he proposed to ensure that it reached its destination without an address to which to write I do not know.

So far as I am aware, he has never spoken to anyone about it, not even to Ballantyne, his bosom friend, no doubt fearing that he would look foolish giving credence to such things. But I know my father. One part of him cannot help but wonder if perhaps there is no trickery and the letter is precisely what it says it is.

The letter from Mr Gibbon he left lying about for a long time, no doubt hoping everyone would pick it up and read it, 'Sir,' wrote the eminent historian, 'your communication pleased me immensely. Your suggestions concerning the astronomical calculations of the Goths I found both persuasive and elegant. I should like, with your permission, to incorporate it into future editions of my history, with full acknowledgement, it goes without saying.' And so on. I would not be surprised if he wrote it himself.

There was a time, when I had the run of the house, when I frequently found my way to his rooms. Once I replaced a cheval glass with an empty frame and hung a skeleton behind it, but as I was not there to witness the effect the pleasure was somewhat muted, and when I returned later, having ensured that he had taken the carriage, the skeleton had gone, and the empty frame, and the glass was back in its place. Now I am debarred from entering his wing of the house I can no longer play such tricks upon him.

I can still watch and see who comes to visit and even go down and intercept them in the drive. No doubt if he learned of it he would stop me doing even that, but so far this has not happened. That is how I became acquainted with Mrs Simmons, the beautiful widow who came to converse with him about Hebrew grammar and the theology of the Eastern Fathers. At first, standing by the side of the drive and letting the carriage pass by, I would merely nod in greeting. But after a while I started to wave to her, and was gratified to see that she leaned forward and even waved back. Then, one day, she stopped the carriage and asked me to accompany her to the gate.

– I am sorry, she said, when I had seated myself and the

coachman had moved the horses on, that you and your father have fallen out.

I felt it would be wisest to say nothing at this point.

– He feels keenly, she said, the loss of your good will.

– Indeed? I said.

– Oh yes indeed, she said. He does not speak of it but I can see that it distresses him deeply.

This was news to me, but I did not make too much of it, knowing that pretty women are liable to make up stories to suit their own purposes. What exactly her purpose was I had yet to find out.

– Your father is a remarkable man, she said after a while.

I nodded non-committally.

– I am sure, she said, looking at you, that you take after him.

I looked at her. There was no denying that she was an attractive woman. Even more so close to than at a distance, which is not always the case with attractive women.

– I have learned so much since I have had the good fortune to become acquainted with him, she said.

– Ah, I said.

– Yes indeed, she said, motioning to the coachman to stop, for we had reached the gate. He is a man of altogether superior intellect and sensibility.

– Indeed, I said.

– Yes, she said. There is a greatness of spirit there which those fortunate enough to be let into the intimacy of his thoughts cannot fail to discern.

She did not want to question me, I thought, only to unburden herself of her passion for him. Yet she had just made it clear that she was acquainted with his views of me, so that I was puzzled as to her motives.

She laid a hand on my arm:

– You understand what I am saying? she asked, looking up into my face.

I did not, but her touch had a curious effect on me.

– Madam, I said, is there any possibility of misunderstanding?

– Alas, she said, where families are concerned there is always such a possibility.

– But you were surely talking, I said, of understanding between the two of us, and so far as I am aware, there are no familial ties between us.

She blushed and I laid my hand on hers, where it still clasped my arm. She made an attempt to withdraw it, but I held firm.

– I have to go, she said wildly. Please release me.

I lifted her hand, which she now made no effort to pull away, and raised it to my lips.

– So that there should be no possibility of misunderstanding, I said, and turned it over and kissed her palm. Then I opened the carriage door and jumped down, walking away quickly into the undergrowth without looking back. I heard the coachman shout to the horses and then the carriage was gone.

I did not see her again for several days, though I watched at the window for sight of the carriage. I wondered if I had frightened her with my boldness, but the memory of her laying her hand on my arm convinced me that I need have no fear, that she had seen something in me to attract her, whether she was aware of it or not. And how right I was. The following day a letter arrived. I guessed it was from her before opening it.

'My dear George,' it said. 'It would give me great pleasure if you would meet me in the copse on the south side of the house close to the great wall tomorrow afternoon at three. Your devoted friend, Angela Simmons.'

It was news to me that she was my devoted friend, for prior to our meeting in the carriage we had never exchanged a word, but if she was pleased to be my friend, then who was I to contradict her?

I was at the copse at half past two, since it was a fine day and I had nothing better to do. I daydreamed, lying on the grass at the edge of the trees and looking up at the pure blue sky. Three o'clock came and went, and then three fifteen and finally three thirty. I had been sitting up for some time, wondering if something had happened to her, or if I had in some way misread her letter, or if perhaps someone had been playing a cruel hoax on me. I did not think he would do a thing like that, he was too taken up with his own life even to think of playing tricks on others. In fact I have to admit that if it was his work I would have to revise radically my view of him.

I was just considering these matters when I heard the sound of running feet and I had hardly time to look up when she had thrown herself down on the grass beside me. She was younger and more beautiful than I had remembered and my heart at once went out to her, but I felt I should make some show of anger at having been kept waiting.

– Dear boy, she said, panting, how can you ever forgive me? There were a thousand and one things to be done before I could free myself for our meeting, and, alas, I could not do them in such a way as to arrive on time. Will you forgive me?

– It is almost an hour after the time you suggested, I said coldly.

– Dear boy, she said, I have apologised already. I throw myself upon your mercy. And she took my hand and kissed it.

I was silent. She let go my hand and lay down in the grass beside me.

– It is a glorious day, she said. Let us not quarrel.

– Who spoke of quarrelling? I said.

– I knew you would understand, she said. You are so like your father. He always understands. He always makes allowances. A poor foolish woman like myself, she said, cannot but feel immensely honoured to have so wise and distinguished a man as him give up his time to instruct her. I cling to his every word, she said. If only I could write it down in my notebook as he speaks, instead of waiting to get home, when of course I have forgotten most of it! But it would not do, would it, to try and write it down as he was speaking? You do not think it would do, do you?

– I have never heard him say anything I ever had any wish to write down, said I.

– Oh you wicked boy, she said, sitting up and tapping my shoulder in simulated petulance. How can you say such a thing? But I know you do not mean it, she went on. You only say it to tease me. You are so like your father, she said, looking down into my face. You have his mouth and eyes too, did you know that?

I looked up into her beautiful eyes but did not respond.

She sighed.

– I am such a foolish ignorant woman, she said. I often wonder why he puts up with me. Of course, she said, rearranging her hair, which had become a little dishevelled what with the running through the trees and throwing herself on the ground and sitting up and tapping my shoulder and all the rest of it, of course he is such a paragon of politeness that he would not dream of stopping me when I ramble on as I too often do. Nor would he dream of showing me the door when I weary him with my perpetual questions. I am not so lacking in self-awareness, she went on, that I do not realise that he often finds my foolish chatter irritable beyond belief, but I have to confess that I sometimes rather enjoy watching him control himself and only chatter on to see whether his self-control will hold or not. I long, she said, for him to let fly at me, to tell me to hold my peace or to call Alfred and ask him to show me the door. But he will not. He smiles and nods, waiting for me to finish and of course I do not finish because I want to see if for once his self-control will let him down. And I have the feeling, she said, that a part of him rather likes this, likes to have me chattering in his room like a little bird, your father, she said, without drawing breath, is a deeply lonely and unhappy man, we must do everything in our power to relieve his loneliness and his unhappiness, though there is something undoubtedly fascinating about such loneliness and such unhappiness, there is a sense of mystery there which one would dearly like to penetrate. Your father, she went on, knows a great deal about everything but there is one thing he knows very little about, one thing a foolish woman perhaps knows more about than he does, and that is himself. There have been times, she said, when I thought I had goaded him beyond endurance, when I thought I had really gone too far and he would show me the door or bar me from his presence in the future. But it has never happened. And I suspect, she said, that my sheer presence, the simple sound of my voice in his ears, does him good, does him more good, I would almost be prepared to say, than all his books and all his wise correspondents. It filled me with such sorrow, she said, when I heard of your estrangement from him. You are, after all, his only close kin, your brother does not count, it would give him such pleasure to know that he had your trust and respect. I am all too well aware of what a difficult man he is and how much your estrangement is due to him, but you must make allowances, his life has been plagued by misfortune and we must do all we can to help him return to himself. Though he occasionally appears cold, she said, I know that deep down he is a man of enormous warmth and love, that if he would only give himself up to his instincts he would discover that life still had much to offer him. I flatter myself, she said, that I have perhaps been able to give him something which had been missing for too long from his life, and that one day, who knows, even his terrible insomnia will leave him and he will be able to let go of his cares, for the duration of the night at least. But he resists me, she said, the devil in him resists me, he knows it would be the saving of him but he will not listen, he does not show it because of his extraordinary politeness, but I can see him hardening his heart, I can see him endeavouring to shut me out, and it has grown worse, not better, she said. He will close his eyes now when I speak and sit so still I do indeed sometimes think that he has fallen asleep in my presence. I chatter on, she said, waiting to see what will happen, I sense that he prefers me to be quiet, but there is a devil in me too and I will not let him be. There can be no doubt, she said, that he is pleased to see me, I can sense it in his manner, but then I sense as well that contrary spirit, welling up inside him, and sense sometimes that he is only waiting for me to finish and be gone. It was not always so, she said. It has grown worse. It has grown much worse, at first I imagined that it was only a question of time, that as we came to know each other better we would find a deeper intimacy, a new ease in each other's presence, for I could tell at once that we were drawn together, that it was only a matter of time, but time has not been kind to us, something has gone wrong, I am too sensitive not to recognise this, though perhaps I am merely impatient, perhaps I have not really allowed time to do its work and wish to hurry it on against its natural inclination. For deep down there is much understanding between us, I sympathise with how he feels and I do not think I flatter myself when I say that it is reciprocal. But it happens that time needs to be given a push, that he needs to be jolted into realising what it is he wants, what it is he needs, going on as we were will do no good, though I learn much from him and will always be grateful to him for what he has taught a poor foolish woman, what he has made her understand about the world and the ideas and the great thinkers and the nature of the spirit.

Throughout the whole of this extraordinary speech I had lain there beside her on the grass, occasionally glancing up at her as she sat above me, staring out into the distance, but most often with my eyes closed, wondering why she was speaking as she was, whether it was to compassionate me towards my father or towards herself, or simply that she had forgotten my presence and was trying to understand something about herself or about him. When she had been silent for several minutes I realised that she would not continue and that it was up to me to take the next step.

What that would be, though, was not easy to see. It was important, I felt, that I not delay too much. But was I to answer her from below, as it were, or to sit up and speak on a level with her, or to stand above her? I decided to sit up, covering her hand with mine as I did so.

– Madam, I said.

Then I was silent and looked into her eyes. She too was silent and looked into mine. What was she now expecting me to do? The next few seconds would prove decisive.

I stood up.

– Madam, I said again. The day grows cold. It is time you were away.

I leaned over and took both her hands in mine and helped her up. We stood thus in the long grass at the edge of the copse for a brief while, uncertain what to do.

– Madam, I said again. Then:

– It is time to find your coach.

I led her, holding her left hand in my right, till we reached the gate. Then I waved her through and she left me and walked unsteadily to where the coach was waiting. She looked round once and I waved. She did not respond, but got quickly in and, with a word to the coachman, they were off.

I had bought myself time. I had not, I felt, made any false move. I would now wait and see how she responded.

Before that could happen, however, fate intervened in the person of my father. The next day he summoned me into his presence. I could see he was agitated. He sat me down in a chair while he himself walked up and down the room.

For a time he did not speak. I waited, confident that I would be able to handle whatever was to come. Finally he said, with that banality which unfortunately seems to overtake all family situations:

– You no doubt know why I have summoned you.

I made a minimal ambiguous gesture, waiting to see how the wind was blowing.

– It has come to my attention, he began, that you and a certain lady of my acquaintance have been seen together.

He was silent again and I waited for him to continue.

– Seen, he said, in a most compromising situation.

He stopped at the window and turned and looked at me.

– You know what I am referring to, he said.

I examined my hands. They were clean, the nails well cut.

– I cannot understand, he said, what led you, and even more what led her, to act in this way.

I turned my hand over and examined the palm.

– You will understand, he said, that after what has happened it will be impossible for me ever to entertain this lady here in my house again.

He resumed his perambulation, stopped again.

– Should you wish to see her, he pursued, you will of course have to do so elsewhere. There can be no question, no question at all, of her ever setting foot inside my gates again.

I sat back in the chair and stared at him. He turned away and resumed his perambulation.

– I presume, he said, I need not say how it pains me to have to sever all links with her in this way.

Did I detect a smile on his face as he said this? He did not seem as agitated as I would have hoped and indeed expected. Yet she was a beautiful and surely desirable woman, and he was no longer young. Examining him objectively for the first time for some considerable while, I did wonder at her apparent infatuation with him. Perhaps to her foolish eyes a little of the aura of Mr Gibbon and Herr Goethe clung to him.

– Nor need I say, he continued, that I hold you personally responsible for what has happened. Is there anything you wish to say in your defence?

Did he regret what had happened or was he secretly rather pleased? It was difficult to say. And did I, who now had the way clear to pursue whatever goal I wished in relation to her, wish to pursue the matter or not? It really was most puzzling. She was a beautiful and attractive woman. Yet something held me back. Was it fear or prudence? And was my feeling towards *him* one of triumph or defeat?

– I repeat, he said, is there anything you wish to say in your defence?

– What would you have me say? I asked.

– That is up to you, he said.

– Then the answer is nothing, I said.

– In that case, he said, the interview is at an end.

He stood by the window and looked out, waiting for me to go. I did not move.

Finally he turned round.

– You understand all I have been saying? he asked.

– Of course, I said.

Then, since he saw I made no move, he himself hurried from the room, leaving me to savour at least this small sure victory.

‖ 7. Ballantyne

Like the majority of men, Captain William Ballantyne had often wondered how he would react to the birth of his first child. The problem was solved for him by the birth of twins. James and Henry were indistinguishable as babies and remained so as they grew up. Even their father had trouble telling them apart. Only their mother never mistook the one for the other.

The Captain was at sea when, a year later, his next child, a daughter, was born. This was perhaps a blessing, for the little girl, though well-shaped in every way, had the misfortune to be born with webbed hands and feet. When the mother was apprised of this she fell into a fit of hysterics from which she did not emerge for forty-eight hours. Her first words, when she had recovered, were to beg the surgeon to do something about the baby's condition. It seemed, though, that there was nothing to be done without some risk to her young life.

– I cannot let the Captain see her like that, she said to the surgeon. He would never survive it.

– Some people, ma'am, the doctor answered, consider such things the mark of good fortune.

But she could not be appeased.

– I cannot let the Captain see her, she said to the nurse.

– Then you had better make sure she is not here when he returns, ma'am, the nurse retorted.

– But what shall I do? the poor woman cried. What have I done to deserve this?

– If you was willing to pay, ma'am, the nurse said, I know of someone who would be willing to raise her.

– Here in this city?

– No, ma'am, far away in the Western Isles.

– I cannot bear to look at her, the poor woman said. Does that make me an unnatural mother?

– What is natural, ma'am? the nurse said.

So the Captain, when he returned, was told the sad news that the child had not survived, and when the little boys were old enough to ask what had happened to their baby sister they were told that she had been taken away to a better place.

The couple had no more children. Whether the spectre of her absent daughter inhibited the mother or whether the twins were deemed posterity enough, it is impossible to tell. Meanwhile, the boys were growing up. Like all identical twins, they found it difficult to distinguish their own boundaries. When James was beaten, Henry suffered; when Henry cut his leg, James bled. When one was absent the other knew exactly what he was doing, and when they were together they had no need to speak to know what each was thinking. As they grew older their parents and teachers tried to keep them apart, feeling that this unnatural seepage of the mind and body of the one into the other did not bode well for their future well-being. The boys did not complain at this, nor did they seem unduly upset, readily forming friendships with others and leading the normal lives of healthy children. Yet when they were not together it was as if a part of them was absent, they would not hear what was being said to them, or would stop suddenly in the middle of a sentence and, when asked what was the matter, appear to have forgotten what it was they had begun to say. Jimmy is returning today, Henry would say to his parents at the breakfast table. No, his father would say, he is not due back till Saturday week. He is returning today, Henry would repeat. Has he sent you some private message? his father would ask. No, sir, I have had no message. Then why do you say he is returning today?

The boy would not answer, and, in due course, James would appear that day. His hosts had suffered a fire, their property had been gutted, no, no one was hurt, but they had sent him home as soon as it was light.

James was the quiet, bookish one, Henry the more outgoing and active. When the time came it was decided that Henry would follow his father into the navy while James would look after the family property. Henry had been at sea for six months when James was overcome one day with nausea, fell to vomiting, could not stand upright and was hurried to bed. He lay there rigid, saying nothing, though showing no further sign of illness, but refusing to move. His parents feared the worst, and, indeed, shortly afterwards news came through that Henry had died at sea, swept overboard in a sudden squall which had threatened to overwhelm the ship. When they broke the news to James he only said: I know, and would not utter another word. He was trying to decide for himself what difference it made that his brother was dead. Since he was and always had been as much his brother as himself, the fact of death was accidental. If he was present to me, was, in a sense, here inside my body with me, when he was in the Azores, he said to himself, is he any less with me now he is at the bottom of the sea?

James had a former school friend, Alan Inglis, who had married an Orkney girl and settled as a farmer on the mainland. Hearing that tragedy had struck his friend he redoubled his annual invitation to visit him and his young family, and this time James accepted. After an arduous journey he arrived at the busy port of Stromness, where Alan was waiting to welcome him.

– You must treat our house as your very own, he said. You must do exactly as you please here.

James thanked him and said he would.

As he had explained in his letter, this was the busy time of the year for Alan, but he had some lively neighbours whose passion was the antiquities of the region.

– They would dearly like to show you everything there is to see, he said.

So he introduced him to Enoch and Sally Gordon, a handsome and charming couple, who soon whisked him off to see the extraordinary chambered tomb at Maes Howe, which had only recently been uncovered, and the striking circle of standing stones known as the Ring of Brogar.

Roughly oval in shape, the mound of Maes Howe measures some 115 feet in the longest diameter and about 24 feet in height. A passage some thirty-six feet in length, carefully lintelled over and paved underfoot, but no more than four feet high, allows the visitor to crawl into the central burial chamber. This measures about fifteen feet square and must have originally been at least sixteen feet in height, but robbers digging in from above had caused the crown of the vault to collapse and a makeshift lower ceiling had been installed when the tomb was rediscovered. Opening on the three sides of the central chamber, in front and to the right and left of the entrance, small square doorways, placed about three feet above the floor, admit one to the actual burial cells, small charnel chambers each roofed by a single slab. The megalithic masonry is quite superb. The flagstones (in the passage more than eighteen feet in length) have all been dressed to an ashlar-like finish, and are fitted together with such accuracy that in some places you cannot push a knife blade into the joints. At each corner of the central chamber, the better to carry the great weight of the corbelled roof, are massive internal buttresses, faced with monolithic slabs no less than nine feet eight inches high.

The effect of this sepulchral chamber upon the visitor, when once he has crawled in and stands upright at the centre, is over-whelming. Clearly, as Sally explained, this had been the family burial place of a great prince – perhaps a precursor of that *regulus Orcadum* of whom Adamnan writes in his *Life of St Columba*. Unfortunately, she explained, Maes Howe had been ransacked by Norsemen in the twelfth century, though in compensation the tomb-robbers had left on the walls – and she held up her lantern to show him – the largest and finest collection of runic inscriptions in the world. What these mean, though, was still a mystery, though several scholars, friends of theirs, were hard at work, trying to break the code. The *Orkneyinga Saga* tells us that Earl Harold and his men 'were in Maes Howe while a snow storm drove over them, and two men among them went mad there; and that caused them much delay', Sally told him. And she pointed out by the flickering light of her lantern some spirited carvings of a lion-like monster, a walrus, and serpent-knot.

James was more interested in the way the light played on her pale sensitive face and restless eyes than on the work of a long-dead Norseman. From the first he had been drawn to her and she, who seemed no longer to have much to say to her husband, a tall morose man with hooded downcast eyes, had addressed herself exclusively to him.

The Ring of Brogar lies in the very centre of the mainland of Orkney. Here, within a shallow fosse, stands an immense megalithic circle, no less than 340 feet in diameter. Twenty-seven of the original sixty stones still stand, of which the tallest rises fifteen feet above the grass. Some are incised with runic inscriptions. The stones are far more slender and elegant than in any of the stone circles of England, and the mystery of the spot is further enhanced by the mere in the centre, in which the stones are reflected, and by the ever-present sea, which, at the nearest point is but thirty or forty yards away.

– Well? Sally said as they stood in the midst of the stones.

Looking at her, silhouetted against the grey skies, James felt that she was asking for more than a response to the site.

– Do you like us?

Was she referring to herself and tall Enoch, or identifying with the slender stones or with the whole bizarre island, with its seaweed-eating sheep, its chambered tombs and dour dark fishermen?

They walked down to the mere together, leaving Enoch lying on the ground beneath one of the stones, gazing up into the sky and chewing on a blade of grass.

– Do you like us?

– Us? he said. All this?

She did not reply.

– I don't know, he said.

– That's honest, she said.

They stood, looking into the unreflecting water.

– Do you want to stay?

He was afraid of offending her, unsure how to respond.

– Will you come on an outing with us to the Bay of Skaill on Saturday? she asked him.

– I'd love to.

– We'll come round for you at eleven.

*

When the hour came she was the only one there.

– Get in, she said, indicating a seat beside her in the trap.

– Where's Enoch?

– He's indisposed.

– Shouldn't you have stayed with him?

– He prefers to be by himself.

She gave the horse the order to start and off they went.

– I've never seen the sky so blue here, he said.

– That's not such a good sign.

– You mean it's going to rain?

– We may get some gales.

He settled down to enjoy the scenery.

– I'm sorry about your brother, she said after a while.

– You know?

– Alan told me.

– Have you lived here long? he asked her.

– No. We only moved here last year.

– From?

– The Western Isles. Do you know them?

– No, he said. Though I've often wanted to visit them.

– Here we are, she said. She jumped down and set to work unharnessing the horse and giving him his nosebag.

– Take out the food-basket, she said, and unpack it down there on the beach.

The bay was fringed with a wide sandy beach, flat as a pancake. He took out a tablecloth and laid it down on the sand, but he had no sooner done that than the wind lifted it up and turned it over. He placed little piles of sand at each corner and quickly took out the plates and the food, but before he had set them out the sand at each corner had been blown over the cloth. He felt it grinding between his teeth.

– It's windier than I'd realised, she said as she joined him.

He busied himself brushing the sand off the cloth.

– It's always windy here, she said. Windy and wet. People who are born here don't seem to distinguish between wet and dry, wind and calm.

– At least it's not raining.

She handed him a bottle and he opened it and poured wine into both their glasses. As he handed her her glass she kept her hand on his for a moment. What am I doing here? he thought. Why have I come?

Despite the wind it was warm in the sunshine and she suggested they have a swim.

– Here?

– You've never been in the sea?

– Not to swim, he said.

– But you can swim?

– No, he confessed.

– I will teach you. Besides, the bay is shallow, you need not swim at all, you know. Only paddle.

– I'd rather watch you.

– That's not allowed. Either we both go in or neither of us does.

– The wind's getting stronger.

– You're afraid of the wind?

Suddenly a more violent gust knocked the glasses over and sent the food flying over the sand.

– You're right, she said. We should at least pack the things up first.

But by the time they had done that the sand was flying in their faces and the waves were crashing in to the shore. Thick clouds, coming up from the west, covered the sun.

– We must find shelter, she said. We can't go home in this.

They packed the things into the trap, fighting now to stay upright in the face of the gusts, which picked up the sand and sent it whirling up into the air, blotting out the sky.

– There's a hut at the end of the beach, she said. We'd better make for that.

She tied the horse up against the wall and they crept inside the hut. Part of the roof was down but one corner was well covered and the walls at least were still standing as they had been built. They pressed down the long grass and sat down next to each other with their backs to the wind.

– It can't be night already, he said, as the fragment of sky they could see darkened.

– It's the sand, she said. It's blotting out the light.

They listened to the wind.

– Close your eyes, she said.

He felt her fingers on the back of his neck.

– Don't move, she said. Not till I tell you.

When he did open his eyes, much later, the sky was quite dark overhead and the wind seemed, if anything, to have grown more violent. His brother was not dead after all, he realised. Somehow, he had survived and got ashore somewhere. Life had started again for him.

He ran his hand down her belly and thighs, bent over and carried on down to her ankles. His hand moved over her foot and his heart froze.

– What's that?

– Skin.

– Skin?

– Just skin. Does it frighten you?

He moved away but she pressed up to him.

– Feel, she said, and laid her hand on his chest.

He touched her fingers. He knew what he would encounter.

– It's not dirty, she said. Ducks have feet like that, don't they?

Harry was living on his island. He drank coconut milk. Perhaps he had married a beautiful islander with long dark hair. He couldn't tell yet. But soon he would know. As soon as he had a bit of time by himself he would know if he was married and exactly what kind of a life he had made for himself on his island.

– Don't they?

– Yes.

– Well then.

Perhaps he had planned it all from the start. Perhaps he had thought he would know.

– What are you thinking?

– I am thinking that my brother is alive.

He must have slept after that because when he opened his eyes again the wind had subsided and daylight had returned. She lay on the grass beside him, her head thrown back, her arms and legs splayed out. He got up, careful not to disturb her, pulled his clothes on and went outside.

The beach was unrecognisable. The smooth expanse of sand seemed to have been churned up by an army. Holes gaped in it and stones had been uncovered on the southern corner, while mounds of sand had piled up on the northern and eastern edges. He walked slowly down to the sea and gazed out at the waters of the bay, now calm once more.

Harry was asleep beneath the moon. As he bent over him he could see his chest rising and falling as he breathed, and he knew for certain now that he was alive, that what he had felt in the hut had not been a mistake.

*

Two days later James Ballantyne left the mainland of Orkney. He told his friend Alan Inglis that he had seen as much as he ever wanted to see. He did not try to get in touch with his new friends, the Gordons, and he did not even stop for long at the family house, but moved on south, clear in his mind that he would make a new life for himself in England. He would become a farmer, he decided. He would clear a space in his head and give himself time to think about his brother, far away on his tropical island, far away yet always close at hand, as close, if not closer, than he was to himself.

8. In the Carriage (2)

Goldberg and Hammond are riding in Hammond's carriage. The day is fine and warm. The two men sit shoulder to shoulder, looking out at the countryside moving slowly past them.

– And what, Hammond asks, are you at work upon now, Mr Goldberg?

– This and that, Goldberg says.

– Always this and that, Hammond says.

– Always, says Goldberg, smiling.

– There is no letting up? Hammond asks.

– No, Goldberg says.

– Not ever?

– I will not say that, Mr Hammond, Goldberg says, smiling again.

– But at the moment you are in the vein?

– There is always something to be done, thank God, Goldberg says.

– You are a learned man, Mr Goldberg, Hammond says. I have been meaning for some time to ask you: What is the reason, do you think, that makes Homer depict Odysseus as an inveterate liar?

– You are thinking of the lies he tells about himself to his loyal swineherd Eumaeus and to his loving wife Penelope?

– I can see, Hammond says, that there are moments when it would be imprudent to tell the truth. What I cannot understand though is why the hero we are meant to admire and sympathise with seems unable to open his mouth without a stream of the most arrant falsehoods pouring out.

 – There are two epithets most constantly associated with
Odysseus, Goldberg says. *Polymētis* and *polytlēmon*: many-wiled
and much-enduring. The two naturally go together. Odysseus has
lived to endure much because he is many-wiled, full of *mētis,* or
cunning. A man more noble than Odysseus, Achilles, for example,
would not have been able to escape so often from the dangers that
beset him on his homeward journey. Yet to endure, for Homer, is
also an active state, as much as to be cunning. It means being able
to repress anger when to give way to it would prove fatal, to
control yourself when to lose control would be dangerous in the
extreme. Achilles and Ajax, even Hector, the heroes of the *Iliad,*
cannot help but give way to righteous anger. To do less would be
shameful in their eyes; it would be to lose face, and nothing can
be worse than that. Odysseus too recognises the virtue of anger
and the shame of its repression. Yet for him there is a higher
imperative, the imperative which overrides even the need not to
feel ashamed. What is that imperative? It is the need to return
home. Does that make him a coward, seeking only to protect his
own skin? After all, the alternatives are held out to Achilles in the
Iliad in stark fashion: to die young, heroically, or to return home
safe and sound and live out a long life. That is no choice at all for
Achilles, at least so long as he is alive, for to spend the rest of his
life shamefully recalling his cowardice would be to condemn
himself to a life of misery. It is true that when Odysseus sees him
in Hades he confesses that he would rather be a slave than a king
among the dead, but in life there hardly seems to him to be a
choice. He knows that if he kills Hector he himself is doomed to
die young, but kill Hector he must, to avenge his beloved
Patroclus. If it had been possible it would have happened, as
someone has said. If the alternative had been possible he would
have chosen it. It was not possible. Even Hector, who will leave
behind him a grieving wife and son, and whose death will ensure
that they end their days as captives and slaves, cannot do otherwise than leave the protection of the walls of Troy and face the
man he knows will end his life. For him too there is no real choice.
Yet the possibility is there, as it is for Achilles. We are aware of the
fact that at a certain moment another possibility was open. That
is what makes the *Iliad* a tragedy. It is different with the *Odyssey.*

Odysseus is ready to use all his wiles and all his powers of endurance, even if it means humiliation, in order to ensure his safe return and, once he is home, the routing of the suitors and the cleansing of his house. The notion of home-coming in the latter poem is bound up with the notion of time: twenty years. Time does not really exist in the *Iliad*, because there the contrast is between a *now* in which it is imperative to act, no matter what the consequences and a *then*, which would be the eternity of a whole life-time of shame, for both Achilles and Hector. But for Odysseus humiliation is *temporary*; the end always justifies the means. By enduring he guarantees his eventual triumph, whether over Calypso, the beautiful nymph who holds him captive, or over the Cyclops, who holds him prisoner in his cave, or over the suitors and their accomplices amongst the household servants: to endure now is a form of nobility, which would have been inconceivable in the *Iliad*, and to endure requires guile, which is only a means to an end.

But what is the end? Is it to return home safe and sound? Is it to save himself? If that were all he would indeed be an Achilles who had chosen the shameful option, Goldberg continues. But the poem suggests otherwise. It suggests that what he is returning to is the love of his wife and the restoration of his house. Our more sentimental age would privilege the first, and Homer certainly does not play this down. When the beautiful Calypso offers Odysseus, at the very start of the poem, the choice of an eternal life with her eternally young and beautiful self, and the temporal life of all mortals with an aged and wrinkled Penelope, Odysseus has no trouble choosing the latter. Or rather, there has never been any question of choice for him. He feels it in his body, just as much as Achilles and Hector feel it in theirs, that any other choice would be a betrayal of that which constitutes his very self. At the same time the act of reuniting himself with Penelope and taking charge of things in Ithaca is the act of wresting the household and its wealth from the suitors and preserving it for Telemachus, his rightful heir. Thus the household, the *oikos,* is as much the hero of the epic as it is of Aeschylus' *Oresteia*, and the point about the household is that it stretches backwards and forwards in time and that it is bigger than any of its constituent parts. Aeschylus, it seems, was a deep reader of the *Odyssey*, for in the epic we already have the antitype to Odysseus and Penelope in Agamemnon and Clytemnestra: Agamemnon returns home after the sack of Troy to his wife and family and household, but what he finds when he gets there is an unfaithful wife and a divided family. 'Unlike Odysseus, Agamemnon… unlike Agamemnon, Odysseus…' is a perpetual refrain in the early portions of the poem. For house and beloved wife cannot be separated. There is the one because there is the other. While Odysseus has been undergoing his adventures on the high seas Penelope and Telemachus have themselves been enduring, have themselves been using all their cunning, in order to preserve the house and its possessions for when their master returns home. As the *Iliad* ends with the burial of Hector's body, so the *Odyssey* ends with Odysseus and Penelope finding each other through the riddle of the bed, which is an integral part of the house itself. Only then does Odysseus sleep soundly. Until that moment his fate is to lie awake, making plans while all the creatures of the earth sleep the sleep of the just. Even the suitors sleep well, befuddled by food and wine, unconscious of the doom that is shortly to overtake them. But, dressed as a beggar and now back in his house, unknown to any but his own son, Odysseus, we are told, tossed from side to side like a sausage being fried by a hungry man, who continually turns it over to make sure it is cooked all over. Though Athena comes to him and brings him sleep at last, it will not be the sort of sleep that refreshes and renews a man, for there is still much to be done.

– You ask me, Goldberg says, why Homer makes Odysseus a liar, and how he can square that with his presentation of him as the hero of his epic. The answer, I suspect, is that only he who holds firmly to a course of action he knows to be right can lie well. *Mētis*, cunning, requires the ability to keep silent when need be, and the ability to lie convincingly when that is required. However, I am sure you are right in suggesting that Odysseus seems to take pleasure in his lies in ways we would perhaps find reprehensible today. But is it not perhaps we who are at fault? asks Goldberg. Do we not have too anxious a relation to truth? Earlier ages, which trusted more in providence than we do, were not afraid of lies, saw them, in fact, as being necessary as speech itself to man in his dealings with others. The source of Odysseus' lies is the same as the source of his cunning and endurance: an energy which is confident in its goal and relishes all challenges. For there is no doubt that Odysseus goes out of his way to seek adventures, whether in the den of the Cyclops or even, disguised, in his own home. The protection of Athena gives him the confidence to scheme, disguise himself and lie. Or perhaps Homer merely calls such confidence the living of a life under the protection of a goddess.

– Odysseus, Goldberg says as the carriage sways along the narrow country roads, reminds me of our own King David, also a liar and a schemer and a much-enduring man, whose strength lies in his confidence. Even at the end, Goldberg says, when he has committed both murder and adultery, when one of his sons has died in infancy and another has led a revolt which drives him into exile and which lead eventually to that son's death, even then David, after much genuine lamentation, picks up the pieces of his life and reigns to the best of his ability till death comes to him in his old age. A Christian conscience may flinch at some of the activities in which David seems to indulge without any evident sense of guilt and remorse, says Goldberg, but the narrative shows no sign of flinching. It merely flows on, as does the narrative of the *Odyssey*, leaving Saul and Uriah and Absalom in its wake, as Odysseus leaves his dead comrades. Neither Odysseus nor David ever contemplates the central Christian question of how to save his soul, for such questions have no meaning for them. Their goals are specific and limited, and they use all their wiles and all their powers of endurance, to achieve them, and both, despite all setbacks, are successful. Athene helps and comforts the one, the God of Israel the other, and the narrative has no doubt that with such help victory is inevitable. It is perhaps only those who are less than confident of the truth who fear, as we do, the indubitable power of lies.

Goldberg is silent and Hammond gazes out of the window at the passing scenery.

– I hope I have answered your question, Goldberg says.

– You have given me food for thought, Hammond replies.

– Did you not want that?

– On the contrary. That is why I ventured to put the question.
They are silent, rocking together to the rhythm of the carriage.
Goldberg takes his watch out of his pocket and examines it.

– Do not fret, Mr Goldberg, do not fret, Hammond says. We will
soon be there.

Goldberg replaces the watch in his pocket and turns to him,
smiling.

9. Sarah

When Sarah was twelve she had a dream. She was lying on her back in a field full of flowers, looking up at the sky and breathing deeply. She remembered the deep breaths long after she had awoken. The sky was blue, cloudless. A light buzzing filled her ears. Then a speckled butterfly floated into her field of vision. She sat up and watched it as it flitted in the air above her. Then it moved on, stopped, turned, and seemed to beckon her. She got up and followed, stepping without effort over the field of flowers. When it got too far ahead of her the butterfly would pause as though waiting, then set off again.

When they got to the edge of the field the butterfly swooped round and began to go back the way they had come. Time after time she followed it this way and that across the field, growing more and more tired, trying now to grasp it, first with this hand and then with that, but it always flew just out of reach.

Now she was too tired to move any further and she lay down on the grass, which was hard and dry, and closed her eyes, to keep out the incessant buzzing, but that only made it worse. She had the feeling that it was swooping down over her and away again. She lay very still and felt it land on her chest, then, sharply, brought her hand down over it, but when she peered under her fingers it was no longer there and she saw it in the air above her, darting this way and that as though to admonish her for her outburst.

Then, before she could rightly understand what was happening, it had swooped behind her and flown straight into her ear.

She shook her head, trying to clear it. She could feel the creature flying this way and that inside it, fluttering against the hard
wall of her skull, but if there was a way out, and there surely must
be since there had been a way in, it did not seem able to find it.

– I've got a butterfly in my head, she said to her brother. It won't
let me alone.

– She's got a butterfly in her head, he said to their father. It
won't let her alone.

– Butterfly? What are you talking about? Goldberg said.

– It's in her head. It can't get out.

– What's he talking about? Goldberg asked his daughter.

– It's true, she said. It flew into my ear and now it can't get out.

– Put your finger in your ear, Goldberg said.

She did as she was told, staring at him tearfully.

– How far in can it go? Goldberg asked.

– This far.

– Well then.

– My finger's not a butterfly.

– No. It's smaller than a butterfly.

– Now I'll have to live the rest of my life with a butterfly in my
head, she said.

– I'm afraid you will, he said.

– Unless it dies first and rots.

– Butterflies don't die, Goldberg said. Didn't I teach you? They
turn into caterpillars.

– No, his daughter said. Caterpillars turn into butterflies.

He put his hands round her head and drew her to him:

– Is it in there? he said.

– Yes, she said. You don't believe me but it's flapping around
against the walls of my skull. It'll flap around till the day I die. I
won't be able to sleep, not ever again, or to think.

– Look on the bright side, Goldberg said. Perhaps it will help
you to think. Perhaps you'll become the greatest thinker of all
time.

– With a butterfly in my head, Sarah said.

10. Control

Westfield's father had wanted many children but had had to make do with only one. He determined to bring the boy up in such a manner that he would be able to face the challenges of a changing world. A man doesn't cry, was his refrain when the child fell and cut his knee. A man learns to control himself, was the basic tenet he reiterated as the boy was sent to bed without food for getting into a tantrum when told he would not be allowed to accompany his father to town the following day or complained that the fishing rod he had been given was not the one he had asked for. With his father the young Westfield tramped over the mountains till he was crying with exhaustion or swam across Scottish lochs so cold the blood froze in his veins and his head ached every time he dipped it in. A man should fear nothing, his father said, but Westfield knew that he would never be able to overcome his fear of his father.

He sought refuge with his mother, and heard his parents arguing over him as he buried his head in her skirts. How can I make a man of him, his father shouted, when you undo all the good work I've done by mollycoddling him like that? You push the child too hard, his mother said. You will break him before you make him. Where did you get such ideas from? his father shouted. I never taught you things like that! Hush, dear, his mother said, you frighten us more than you realise with your shouting. Is he a boy or a girl? his father said, in a quieter tone. It makes no difference, his mother said. He is a human being. Where do you think I'd be if I hadn't been trained to endure? his father said. Where did you get that idea, woman? Do you think nurture counts for nothing? Do you think education counts for nothing?

Culture, said his father. Cultivation. The ploughing of the fields. Without the plough we would be picking berries off trees still. And much happier we would be for it, his mother said. Much happier? his father shouted, his face purple with rage. Much happier? Do you know what you're saying, woman? Do you want me to turn you out of the house and let you find your food in trees? Is that what you're saying? I'm not saying anything of the sort, his mother said, I merely wish you to treat the boy as a child and not as a footsoldier. My dear, his father said, have I ever had anything but his best interests at heart? No dear, his mother said, but I wonder if you set about things in the best way. I think you should let me be the judge of that, his father said.

Nevertheless, though his father had to be obeyed, his mother provided him with a refuge. He knew he could not rely on her to protect him but he drew comfort from her presence.

What does a man do? his father asked him. Control himself. When? At all times. Why? Because that is what distinguishes him from the beasts. Good, his father said.

When his father was away his mother let him read in the library for as long as he liked. Sometimes she would knock on the door and ask him if he wanted to come out for a walk. He was so grateful to her that he always said yes, even when he would really have preferred to finish the book he was reading. Look at the squirrel, his mother would say, or, Look, the bluebells are out.

One day his father announced: Your mother and I are going away for a few days. Mrs Dummit will look after you while we are gone.

He glanced quickly at his mother for a denial, but none came. He could not believe it. They had never left him. She had never left him. It was impossible.

His mother did not speak to him. She turned her head away as though she knew what she had done. Or perhaps she didn't know. Perhaps he had misunderstood everything. Perhaps it was the most natural thing in the world for her to go away with her husband and leave him behind.

That was when he learned that his father had been right after all. That was when he understood why it is a man must learn to control himself. He could not believe that she had betrayed him like that, but he had to face the fact that she had. The two of them went away and he was left alone with the housekeeper. He vowed never again to allow himself to be put in a position where he was not in control. When his parents came back his mother sensed that he had turned away from her and she could not understand why. She thought he was sulking because she had gone away, but the real reason was that he had learned to trust his father and not her. That moment, Westfield felt, marked the end of his childhood and the start of his adult life. ▮

11. Containers

A shelf in a shallow recess, above which is a cupboard with two small doors, one of which is partially open, but not enough to allow one to see inside, the other firmly shut. Each door is fastened to the frame by two elaborate metal hinges, which extend to within an inch or two of the further edge and which, at the point of juncture, take up about a quarter of the vertical length of the door. In the middle of each door, an inset panel with a flower pattern carved into the wood. In the centre, a massive lock, also metal, with a ring attached a little below the keyhole and to the left as one looks at it. Because this door is partially open the light plays on the panel and brings out the colour of the wood, in contrast to the dimness of the recessed space below and the darker texture of the wood of the closed door on the right hand side. This one identical to the other, except that it is shut tight, the bolt in place and the key in its hole. A large bunch of keys hangs below the metal surround, reaching almost to the arm of the hinge. The two doors, clearly mirroring each other when they are shut, establish a play of similarity and difference now one is partially open.

Below, on the shelf and hanging from hooks in the recessed wall above it, eleven objects: two books, a round box, seven bottles and jars, and a fruit. They are disposed in the following fashion: at the bottom, on the left, flush with the left hand wall, lies a large book bound in dark leather, its white pages facing us. Two straps are visible, designed to keep it closed, though only the left hand one performs this function, while the right hand one is loose and folded back over the top cover. Where the half-open door above takes up about one third of the upper half, the book takes up almost exactly half of the width of the shelf. On it stands a greenish glass jar with a rounded belly and a narrow neck. A quarter of its base rests on the left side of the first, closed strap, three quarters on the other side. Just above the strap, in the lower left hand portion of the jar's belly a window seems to be reflected, and, probably, the rest of the room, though, because of the dimness of the shelf, it is impossible to be certain. A whitish stopper is partially inserted into the neck. Next to it, a few inches away and covering the second, unfastened strap, is a round box, made of thin wooden strips, its lid in place. Balanced on top of it is the fruit, probably a coarse-skinned lemon, the light bringing out its grainy texture. Next to the book and obscuring much of its top edge, stands a white jar with an elegant lid rising to a point. It is round, narrowing slightly towards the base. Along the rim of the lid and the middle and bottom of the jar runs a delicate pattern of red lines. Between the lines on the lid, a series of reversed epsilons, the middle member of each pushing forward to touch the rounded back of the adjacent one. Below, three fainter lines can be made out. In the middle, also divided by two firm red lines above and below which are three thinner lines, is a word in a beautiful, very elaborate but indecipherable script, while a fragment of another word is just visible on the left, suggesting that the text runs round the jar. It is set slightly back from the edge of the shelf, so that its base is invisible. Next to it, just touching it and leaning at a diagonal against the right hand wall, is another book, less massive than the first, with a fine red binding embossed with metal studs. More studs hold the two straps firmly in place. The two books thus mirror the two doors above, the one ajar, the other locked.

Returning to the left hand side, between the bottle and the lemon hangs a brown jar, one of whose handles is clearly visible, the other just discernible in the gloom. It is to these handles that the strap which attaches the jar to a hook fitted into the wall is tied, forming a triangle enclosing a green stopper which does not plunge directly into the neck of the jar but into a white paper ruff. Next to it, a little higher and hanging down just to the right of the lemon, a jar or bottle encased in a yellow wicker basket with a twisted wicker handle attached to the top edge, which is covered with a dark green cloth. Next to that, and hanging almost directly above the elegant white box, a clay water-bottle, whitish-brown, the marks of the potters' wheel very visible. Its rounded belly is offset by two handles, which give it the appearance of having square shoulders, above which rises a small neck topped by a lid of some dark material. The leather strap by which it hangs passes under the armpits, and round the neck a label is attached, though the writing on it is too small to be decipherable. To its right, on a higher hook, hang two dark angular containers. The first, long and narrow, almost touches the top corner of the red book; the other, just visible in the gloom, is much smaller, roughly a third of its size. Both are attached to their hooks by means of three reddish-brown threads sewn into the fabric of the two containers and which, in the case of the first, form a belt some two thirds of the way down, clearly dividing its surface into two unequal sections. ▌

12. The Second Mrs Westfield

My Dear Jane,

He's arrived!

I wore my blue dress with the lace collar and the long sleeves, the one you admired so much and even admitted to being just a tiny bit envious of, and the new white shoes, and thank goodness I'd washed my hair the previous day, because he was early. He's strikingly handsome, tall and dark with deep set eyes and he looks so sad, so sad. No, it's not true. He's a bit of a disappointment, as a matter of fact, with a big puffy face and an awkward walk – but at least he's male! I could see at once that I'd made an impression on him, he kept following me about with his eyes – pale blue and not bad, as a matter of fact. He doesn't say much and is most polite to everyone, and I think just a tiny bit shy, which is sweet. Let us, however, wait and see.

Your loving siren.

My Dear Jane,

What a bore! What a dreadful bore! I took him for a walk yesterday and he didn't say a thing. At home he reads a lot and stares out of the window a lot. He doesn't know how to play games, he's frightened of horses, and hardly seems interested in me at all! He asks me the names of flowers and seems perfectly happy to tag along behind, but he doesn't really know how to do anything. And to think I had lain awake all night waiting for him to arrive! It is a fact of life that our hopes are never realised and that reality never lives up to our imaginings. So pity

Your poor siren.

My Dear Jane,

Are you enjoying your summer? I'm not enjoying mine, I can tell you. True, he's begun to show an interest in me, but, if anything, that only makes things worse.

To give you an example. Yesterday on our walk I lay down in the long grass by the little copse and he lay down at a respectful distance from me. When I grew bored with looking up at the sky I tried tickling him with a blade of grass. Don't do that, he said, it tickles. Of course I went on. Don't do that, he said again. I enjoy tickling you, I said. Don't you enjoy being tickled? No, he said. So I fell on top of him and tickled him properly, in the ribs and under the arms, and he started to scream and thrash about, and finally he grabbed my hands and held my wrists together so that I couldn't tickle him any more. Then, still holding my hands, he said: Sorry. Just like that: Sorry. Why are you sorry? I said. To have to hold you like that, he said. Then let me go, I said. If I let you go you'll tickle me, he said, and I don't like that. Then you're not sorry, I said. Yes I am, he said. I'm sorry to have to hold your hands like this. Our faces were about a foot apart, so I leaned forward and licked his nose. What are you doing? he said, starting back, but still keeping hold of my hands. Licking your nose, I said. Why? he said. Have you ever heard of anything so silly? Because I want to, I said. That seemed to take him aback. So much so in fact that he abruptly let go my hands and just sat and stared at me with those watery blue eyes of his. Of course that left me feeling pretty foolish, so I just turned away from him and said: Shall we go on? Yes, he said, jumping up. So we went on. But after a while he reverted to it. Why did you lick my nose like that? he asked. Because I wanted to, I repeated. But why did you want to? I just did, I said. Then we walked on in silence for a while, but he wouldn't let it alone. But why? he asked. Why? And just before we reached the house he said: Tell me honestly, why did you do that? What? I said. What you did. What did I do? You know what you did. No I don't, I said, teasing him. You know, he said, when I held your hands. I can't remember, I said. What did I do? You licked my nose. Did I? I said. Don't you remember? he said. No, I said. You must remember. No, I said, I've completely forgotten. And with that we entered the house.

Your ever so intensely bored siren.

My Dear Jane,

I do hope you're having a better time than I. Now he drags
about after me and I have a terrible time trying to avoid him. I'm
busy, I say, I can't go for a walk just now. Later then? he asks.
Perhaps, I say. And later he materialises again and suggests a walk.
I don't feel like it, I say. I have a headache. Then I'll go by myself,
he says, and stands there. Go on then, I say. So, eventually, he
goes. It is a fact of life that when our wishes are granted they are
no longer what we wish.

Mama pesters me with, You asked to have him to stay, you
couldn't wait for him to arrive, now be nice to him. How could I
know he'd be like that? I say to her. He's a perfectly nice boy, she
says. And so well-mannered. I will not have you being rude to him.

I can assure you it's not much fun being an only daughter.

Your most intensely bored siren.

My Dear Jane,

How I envy you! Nothing happens here at all. We are adrift on
life's raft in a windless sea.

He goes his own way and I go mine. I've started riding again
and am enjoying it more than I used to. He no longer asks me to
go for walks with him. In fact, apart from mealtimes, I rarely see
him. It's all so boring I have begun to spy on him for want of
anything better to do. I follow him from a distance and find a
curious pleasure in knowing that I myself am not being seen. He
stops quite often and sits on a stone or a tree-stump and writes
things down in a little notebook. I would dearly like to get hold of
that notebook. I wonder if he is writing poems about someone we
both know. When he has finished he puts it back in the inside
pocket of his jacket. Unfortunately he is never without his jacket
and never takes it off. Then he gets up again and walks on, sometimes very slowly, looking down at the ground, sometimes
quickening his pace so that I have some difficulty keeping up with
him. Once or twice he looks round as though sensing that he is
being watched, and once the other day he stared and stared at the
bushes behind which I was hiding. I thought he was going to come
and discover me, but after taking a step or two in my direction, he
seemed to change his mind and turned round and walked on.

There is something rather intriguing about following someone about and seeing them when they think they are alone. Even someone as boring as he is. I keep wondering if he will do anything *shaming*, but you can be sure he won't. All he will do is loll about and write things in a notebook and then lie down in the grass for so long I really think he's fallen asleep. It's such a bore, but what else is there to do? At least you have plenty to keep you amused. So think of

Your unhappy siren.

My Dear Jane,

I decided I had to get that notebook and see for myself. The question was: How? As I think I told you, he always keeps it in his jacket pocket and is never without his jacket. However, I reckoned there must come a time when he would take it off: when he went to bed! Watching his door after he had gone to his room for the night I noted that he kept the lantern lit for a good while and deduced that he must be reading or writing in his notebook, either at his desk or actually in bed. Was there any way to get hold of it then? To creep into his room when he was asleep would be dangerous, and in the dark I would not know where to look, even if I took the risk and even if he kept his door unlocked. And if he woke up and found me in his room he might get the wrong idea, or even, I wouldn't put it past him, start to scream and so wake the household and then what would happen?

Instead what I decided to do was this. I am naturally a light sleeper and my room is directly opposite his. I went to bed, leaving my door slightly ajar. If he got up early in the morning to take a stroll in the park before breakfast there was a chance that he would leave his notebook behind and I would be able to slip into his room and find it before he returned.

My plan seemed excellent and I went to bed full of anticipation. I must have fallen asleep very quickly, for the next thing I knew I had woken in the dark and something was moving about in my room! I lay there with my eyes closed, listening, my heart beating, but I must have made a noise on waking up, because I could sense that whoever was in the room had stopped moving. Of course I knew at once who it was. He must have seen my door ajar and crept in to look at me!

I opened my eyes and strained to see in the dark, but it was pitch black.

It was then that I did something quite silly. I should of course have waited to see what he would do, but instead I said, very quietly: Is that you, Toby? Everything was silent. Toby? I said again, but there was no more response this time. I waited. Finally I could bear it no longer. I said: I know you're there, Toby. But that didn't elicit any response either. Then, very quietly, he began to edge towards the door. I heard it creak a little as he opened it wider, and then he was gone.

What do you think of that?

Your loving siren.

My Dear Jane,

I'm dying to tell you what happened after the mysterious invasion of my room. I tried to catch his eye all through the following day, but he was clearly embarrassed and ignored me, or pretended to. However, as you know, I am not one to take that sort of thing lying down.

I was more determined than ever to get hold of the notebook, and I got my chance sooner than I expected. I had gone up to my room after luncheon to fetch a book, leaving him and the rest of the company downstairs. As I passed his door I gave it a little push and it opened. I stepped inside and quickly surveyed the contents of his room. There were some books on the table by his bed and I went forward eagerly to see if it was among them. Alas, it was not there. I turned and saw more books on the table by the window. But on my way to examine those my foot struck something which went sliding across the floor. I bent to pick it up and found I was holding what I had been after. One glance inside was enough to confirm that it was the notebook. In a moment I had left his room, closed the door behind me and shut myself up in my own room.

Alas, I have to confess that all my manoeuvres, all the risks I had taken, had been an utter waste of time. There was not a single word about me in the whole book! True, there were fragments of poems of which I was clearly the inspiration, but they were so inept, and so little finished that I cannot regale you with any.

Apart from that there were sketches of trees and flowers, and the most pretentious speculations you ever read on life and mankind and the nature of the universe, viz.: The sun and the stars care little for any individual life; they have seen too many flourish and perish. And: Ask a blind man to describe a tree and he will need to feel it all over; ask a sighted man to do the same and what will his actions be? Can you conceive of anyone writing such stuff? Does it not make your head whirl?

I wonder now whether he will ask me if I have seen his note-book or simply pretend that nothing has happened?

It is a fact of life that those who look into what is not meant for their eyes will never find there what they were hoping to find.

Your ever resourceful siren.

Dear Jane,

Well, he has gone and I am heartily thankful.

He did surprise me somewhat the next day when he came up to me as I stood alone by the window watching the rain fall, and held out his hand. I looked at him enquiringly and he said: Give it back, please. What? I said. You know what, he said. I don't, I said, what are you talking about? Are you not going to give it back? he asked, looking into my eyes. I stared back at him. I am good at that sort of thing, and he soon dropped his own eyes. My door is open, he said. You will put it back in the next half hour. I do not have the faintest idea what you are talking about, I said. In that case, he said, there is nothing more to be said. And he turned on his heel and walked away.

You can imagine my dilemma. I did not care a fig for his silly notebook, but if he were to raise the issue with Mama it might lead to more trouble than it was worth. Was it not simpler to do as he had suggested? I was heartily sick of the whole thing and wished only that the time would come for him to depart.

I did not know where he had gone, so I went up to my room and dug the notebook out from under the mattress where I had hidden it. His door was partially open, so I went in quickly, deter-mined to leave it on the desk and get out.

Imagine my surprise when, having replaced the book on the desk and preparing to make my exit, I heard a voice saying: Don't go. I looked round. He was sitting in the window seat, his face in shadow. I did not know what to do. Come and sit, he said, motioning me to a chair next to him. I was so taken aback, since I had assumed he would be gentleman enough to absent himself while I performed my embarrassing task, that I did as he said and sat down where he indicated. So we stayed, him not taking his eyes off my face, me, I am sorry to say, looking down at the floor. Finally, since he seemed unwilling to say anything further, I looked up at him. It was now he who was looking at the floor, his big puffy face all red and his hair looking as though he had been dragged through a hedge. Well, I said finally, if you have nothing to say to me I will leave you. I stood up and at once he was standing next to me and had fastened his arms round me. What do you want? I said, and found myself beginning to laugh, he looked so crestfallen. What do you want? I said again. Let me go. He did so at once, and his arms hung helplessly at his sides. To see what he would do I took his right hand in both of mine and brought it up to my lips. Then I took hold of his little finger and brought it to my mouth. He said nothing. I put his finger in my mouth and licked it. At that he fell upon me and began to kiss my neck, uttering strange sounds as he did so. I jumped back and smoothed down my dress. What are you doing? I said. I thought – he said. I care nothing for what you thought, I interrupted him. Then I turned round and headed for the door. I reached it without his having made a move, and stopped, my hand on the latch. But he would not come after me and so I opened the door, stepped outside and closed it again behind me.

That afternoon he was gone! Thankfully I now have the house to myself again. And now tell me, my dear Jane, what you have been doing with yourself in the course of the last week.

You ever loving siren.

*

My Dear Angela,

What a bore! Nothing to do all day but help Mama with her sewing and dream of the lovely time I had with you. I don't seem to want to look at the sky and the trees and haven't taken Milly out for ages. The days stretch ahead and I wonder what will become of me! Please write at once and give me news of yourself and you know who.

Your disconsolate siren.

My Dear Angela,

Things are looking up. There is a wonderfully handsome gardener newly employed who makes no effort to hide his interest in me. When I pass by he puts down his spade and folds his arms and just stares. I pretend not to notice, but I am afraid even I find myself blushing under the intensity of his dark eyes. I have watched him at work from the window of my room and when there is nothing to distract him he goes to it with a rare intensity. I like that in a man. I like the feeling of dogged concentration, as though all else had been banished from his mind. It gives a kind of added value to his interest in me when I pass. Sometimes he stretches out on the grass under a tree and seems to fall asleep with just the same sort of single-mindedness with which he appears to do everything. It makes one want to enter the very skin of a such a person, so different from the bulk of common humanity.

Will I be able to do so? Wait for the next instalment from

Your ever loving siren.

My Dear Angela,

It has happened!

I stopped in front of him and looked straight into his eyes. It was like staring down into two pools of black water. I didn't know what to say. Finally I said: Why do you look at me like that?

He went on looking at me, not a flicker of expression on his face. I waited and he waited. It became a battle of wills. Then, when he realised I was not going to give in and either ask again or turn away, he said: I don't know, Ma'am.

I'm not sure what I'd been expecting, but I have to confess I was disappointed. Not with his voice, which was deep and warm, like his eyes, but with the inanity of the remark. For how was I to respond? In effect he had cut off the possibility of any further exchange between us. I walked on. To tell the truth, I was not struck by the barrier that had been erected between us by the inanity of his response till I got to my room. However, from another point of view one could say that the ice had been broken. And how much more honest an answer of this kind is than some brash and aggressive reply, such as: Because I like to. Do you not think so?

Your ever resourceful siren.

My Dear Angela,

You will no doubt want to know more about the development of my relationship with Jim.

I have to say that even I hesitated as to the next step. I went on watching him from my window and he went on working and resting with the same intense, self-contained manner as I had noted in him from the start. I decided that there was nothing for it but to confront him again. So, when I had made sure no one was about and that he was at work in a sufficiently remote corner of the grounds, I took a stroll in that direction. This time though he did not put down his spade or hoe or whatever it was and fix me with his gaze. On the contrary, I felt him withdraw more and more into himself as I approached. Finally, I stood in front of him. He went on working, for all the world as if I was not there.

Finally I addressed him. What's your name? I asked him.

Jim, he said, reluctantly, I felt, almost sullenly. And went on working.

Have you been working here long? I asked him.

He must have sensed that I would not let him be until he had stopped his work and faced me. So he did. He leaned on his hoe and looked into my eyes. Not long, he said.

And before that? I asked.

He shrugged his shoulders.

I sat down on the grass and motioned him to sit beside me, but he either mistook my gesture or decided that he would prefer to remain standing. Won't you sit down for a moment? I asked him. No, Ma'am, he said. I have work to do.

Was it shyness? Or something else? Men are such mysterious creatures, dear Angela, but that is what makes them so fascinating.

I felt a little silly, sitting there by myself while he went on with his hoeing, so I got up and brushed the grass off my dress and said: In that case I'd better let you get on with it.

He made no reply but went on as though absorbed in his work. I was gratified, though, to see a flush spread across his neck.

Goodbye, I said to him.

He made no reply, and that, dear Angela, is where we left it.

You can imagine my feelings!

Your ever loving siren.

Dear Angela,

You don't know what's happened! That swine Jim Roberts has complained to Mama! He has gone behind my back and told her I was interfering with his work. Well, how vindictive can you get? The truth of the matter is that men are absolute cowards. I have been forbidden to go near him. As if I cared! They make me sick, the whole lot of them.

Your utterly exasperated siren.

*

My Dear Helena,

Guess what? Yes, you have guessed it.

Your ecstatic

Sirena.

My Dear Helena,

You will all get a formal invitation in due course, but this is just to tell you that the happy event is due to take place on 23 June.

I cannot tell you how sweet he is. And so handsome. We are both in the seventh heaven. Is that the heaven of Saturn? Does the term refer to the Golden Age?

I haven't slept a wink these last few nights, as you can imagine. I lie in bed and think how lucky I am the whole night long.

Your over the moon

Sirena.

My Dear Helena,

I should have written to you ages ago to thank you for the wonderful present. But there has been so much to do since we returned. I am having the house completely redone, so as to fit in with our own exact wishes. It is all going to be quite exquisite, you wait and see.

I was sorry to hear about Edmund. Men are swine. Except for mine. I adore him, from the tips of his toes to the curls of his beautiful head. I know some people find him rather quiet, but then I more than make up for that, don't I? He says my voice makes him think of honey. Is that not charming?

He approaches! I must stop.

Your loving

Sirena.

My Dear Helena,

It's happened! What? You can guess what. Of course you can. I thought the sickness must be a presage and indeed it was. It will be a boy and called William of course after his father. You will be his godmother, will you not? And then you will have to visit as often as you can. Let us hope the house is ready by the time HE arrives.

S.

My Dear Helena,

I hardly have the courage to write these lines. The most terrible thing in the world has happened. I have lost the child. Oh, I have learned so much in the past few days! To think of a whole life with all its attendant joys and sorrows gone before it had even begun. I have been crying without cease and do not know how to pick up the pen to say these few words to you now. Think of me, dear Helena, and think of dear William. But we must put ourselves in the hands of God and resign ourselves to His will. In His will is our peace.

Pray for us, dear Helena, pray for us.

S.

My Dear Helena,

Your letter brought me such comfort. And time too is doing its job. Mourning is necessary but life must go on. This episode has brought us closer together and will knit us together in the future. Of that I am convinced.

Your ever loving
Sirena.

My Dear Helena,

So much time has passed since you wrote. I have to say that I have been in no mood to write. To tell you the truth it has been a difficult time. If it was not for the great and enduring love between us I do not know what I would have done. He is a difficult man. The fact is, life is hard, but pain it is that forges our souls.

Forgive the brevity of this letter, my heart is too burdened to write.

S.

My Dear Helena,

As you will have gathered from my previous letter, all has not been well here. Indeed, that is an understatement. Who could have foretold that this is what would happen? I ask myself if I am to blame, and have to answer that I am not. Except in my foolish gullibility. As you will have gathered from my previous letter, certain things have occurred which have forced me to revise all my previous views. I do not know how I could have been taken in as I was. And it has, it seems, been going on for some considerable time. It is taking all my resourcefulness to come to terms with it.

Your ever loving
S.

My Dear Helena,

I left that hateful house on Sunday and have been here at Papa's for the last few days. I could not go on being party to such deceit and hypocrisy. His parting shot sank him even lower in my esteem than he had already fallen. He accused me of being the one who was at fault, said that it was I who had ruined our marriage and that he could not wait for me to quit his sight. The shame of it. I felt quite shrivelled up and unable even to look at myself in the glass. What have I done to him except to give him love? And what has he done for me except to shame and humiliate me? This has been going on for some considerable time, but I have tried to hide it from the world and even from myself. Now it is out I begin to feel better already, and think of all that has happened as a kind of nightmare from which I am at last awakening. Though I still cannot come to terms with the fact that I, who had so much love to give, should have been treated in this shabby way. I had always thought he was mean, and suspected him of being a liar, but I never thought he would behave in this way. I look at myself in the glass and ask myself how such things could have happened to me, how all my good will and all my efforts, could have been repaid in this way. The fact is that we are alone in the world but will never admit it to ourselves.

When I am recovered I would dearly like to visit you. Meanwhile, have pity on

Your poor Sirena.

*

My Dear Anne,

A very strange thing has happened. My cousin Toby has come back into my life. We had not seen each other since we were children, and warmed to each other immediately. It is so strange seeing him before me now and seeing him as he was twenty years ago, sometimes I see two distinct people and sometimes the two merge into one. He is mourning the death of his wife, who passed away suddenly a few months after they were married. Papa invited him over and he must have liked what he saw because he has been back several times since. I think the fact that I too have been through so much helps me understand him and he is grateful for that. It is a fact of life that suffering, if it does not ennoble, at least makes us more responsive to the sorrows of others.

If I can help him at all to overcome his sorrows I will feel that my life has been worthwhile.

Your loving
Sirena.

My Dear Anne,

He has asked me to marry him. From the moment he appeared in my life I knew that this would be the outcome. We have so much in common and could be said, after all, to have known each other for over twenty years. We are both people who have been dealt vile blows by Life and so we do not perhaps expect too much from the other. That surely is the basis for a happy marriage.

Your happy
Sirena.

My Dear Anne,

I told you I was happy in my last letter but I don't think I conveyed to you the degree of my joy. My body does not seem to be made of solid flesh, it seems to melt and flow outwards into the world, as if I was all heart and nothing else. At least that is how it seems to me. That makes me very vulnerable, like a snail out of its shell, but it also makes me feel as I have never felt before. Perhaps there is some justice in the world after all, and those who suffer much are also destined to have much joy.

He sits, holding my hand, and lets me prattle on, looking all the while into my face. I know the sound of my voice soothes him and that slowly he is forgetting his beautiful dead wife of eleven weeks and beginning to live again in the present, in our new present. We are both starting to thaw in the fire of our new-found love.

Your contented
Sirena.

My Dear Anne,

Our baby boy was born yesterday and you will hardly believe how much he resembles his father. The same proud holding of the head, the same blue eyes, the same set mouth. With his arrival the horrors of my past life have all fallen away, and I am as one made new. I cannot tell you how good Toby has been to me these past few weeks, how he has sat by me and comforted me in my fits of irrational emotion and even tears. Yes, I can confess to you that I have cried a great deal these past few weeks, not out of sorrow and not out of joy, but as though a torrent had been building within me for the past several years and it had to be released in order for life to go on. Who would have thought the old woman had so much salt water within her? But it is as though now that has all come out, and the baby boy as well, I have returned to my true self and can face the future unencumbered. What I have been experiencing in the last days is deeper than joy, deeper even than sorrow, it is quite the deepest thing that it can fall to the lot of a human being to experience. I am humble in the face of that, I mentally go down on my knees to thank whatever powers there be for allowing me to experience it.

My heart is too full to go on, though there is so much to say.

Your fortunate

Sirena.

My Dear Anne,

You ask me why I haven't written for so long. Clearly you do not have two young children to look after. And two boys at that. It is true that the baby is goodness itself, it even worries me sometimes that he cries so little, but Gerald is adorably wild and needs an eye kept on him at all times. Poor Toby cannot cope with it all and withdraws into himself, so that this too requires a constant effort on my part, to keep him happy and amused. As a result I am worn thin with exhaustion, but nevertheless I go on, finding ever new sources of energy and goodwill in my depleted body. You will understand from this that I have little time or energy left over to maintain my correspondence as I ought or to satisfy the demands of friendship. However, I am sure that those who call themselves my friends will understand and bear with me. It is a fact of life that we human beings have only a limited capacity and that we can never fulfil all the demands life makes on us.

Your ever loving

Sirena.

My Dear Anne,

I thank you for your kind letter, which was so full of under-standing of our great sorrow. Little Simon it seems will never be a normal human being. Despite all that the doctors have tried to do the sad truth is that they are helpless. I had thought, since I felt I understood what he said, that in time others would come to do so too, but I have to admit now that this will never be. And though he is a healthy enough child, this fatal lack of speech means that he will be forever cut off from the world. And in recent months he has turned on his mother as well, throwing tantrums when I try to reason with him and at times banging his head against the wall, at others withdrawing into silence and passivity. His poor brother is as baffled as the rest of us, and complains to me frequently that Simon has broken his toys or refuses to play with him. In natural frustration he has even tried to do him bodily injury. I have had to reprimand him, though I understand him so well, and he has promised to be good. Their father retreats further and further into the world of his library, and will not or cannot help. It is a fact of life that the blows of fate affect different people in different ways. We must try to understand those who have not the resilience to react. Thank God that I at least have the willpower to fight unto the last. But even I at times find the demands made upon me by all that has happened almost too much to bear. The knowledge that there are good friends to support me is of enormous importance.

Your loving friend
Sirena.

My Dear Anne,

Is it possible that a human being can suffer as much as I do? Is it my optimism and my trust in the essential goodness of human beings which has brought me to this pitch? The signs were there from the start and I should have known better than to trust one who had been so callous and indifferent as a youth. Is it my fault then that I married him? Now he shuts himself away from me and will not see me. I have tried to reason with him, to beg him, for the sake of the children, to behave in a more civilised manner, but he will not respond. The little one, thank God, will never be able to grasp the depth of his father's callousness, but Gerald is old enough to understand. He asks no questions but everything he says testifies to his powerful hatred of this man who has tricked and deceived me at every turn. Sadly, and for reasons which I cannot understand, this tragedy, which should have brought us closer, has led to his treating even me, his adoring mother, as a stranger. There are times, my dear Anne, when I give way to despair, but you know my strength of character. After all, though I offered him everything and opened my innermost heart to him as I have to no one else, he has done his utmost to crush and destroy me. But I will not be destroyed. If he wishes to have nothing more to do with me I will respond in kind. Nothing he can do will crush my indomitable spirit.

Your loving friend
Sirena.

My Dear Anne,

You ask me how I do, and the answer is, well enough. I have acquired a horse and have taken to riding out every morning before breakfast. I do not sleep much, but the hour or two I spend in the saddle every morning makes the day that follows tolerable. The nights are worse. It is then that my anger rises and my resentment of the way I have been treated. The feel of the wind in my face and the powerful beast beneath me does much to dissipate this, so that by the time I return to my silent and empty rooms I have found again some of my old resilience and equanimity. Perhaps in time I will not need the horse as I do now, but for the moment he is my saviour. When my life closes in on me and I am reduced to being a single point of anger and despair, I think of those morning rides and my heart brightens. I write this so that you will cease to worry yourself about me. One day we will meet and laugh at it all, of that I am sure. But I cannot at present conceive of such a day.

Your loving friend
Sirena.

13. Sinclair

Whenever Goldberg thought of his friend Isaac Sinclair, his heart grew heavy. A promising, if somewhat sentimental poet, Sinclair had earned his living as tutor to several aristocratic youths. His fiery temper and passion for perfection had not been exactly what most parents were looking for, and he had frequently been asked to move on. Finally he had landed up with a family where the mother was as idealistic as he was and the father away on business for much of the time. For a few months all went well, and Sinclair wrote to say how considerate his employers were, how well his writing was progressing and how – for the first time in his life – he felt at peace. Mrs——, he wrote, understands both my needs and my concerns, the boy is no fool, and the house and grounds are utterly conducive to peace of heart.

Too conducive, perhaps, for soon Sinclair and the mistress of the house began to realise that theirs was turning into something more than friendship. Sinclair sensed that he would have to leave again, this time not because of any incompatibility but quite the contrary, because they were all too compatible. He tried to make light of the break, but his friends sensed that something decisive had happened to him. His adolescence was over. His life as a man had begun.

One result was that he began to write more and better poetry than before. Sometimes he adopted a tone of calm resignation, of world-weary wisdom:

In younger days in the mornings my spirit soared,
  I wept at night-fall; now that some years have passed,

>   Though doubting I begin each day, yet
>   Always its end is holy and peaceful.

At other times he seemed to speak more frankly and directly about his torments and their cause:

>   Bliss of the heavenly Muse, who even the elements once
>   Did reconcile, come and assuage now the Chaos of Time!
>   But the more beautiful world, the sun of the spirit, is fallen
>   Now in frost of the night quarrelling hurricanes rage.

To his friends he seemed to have come into his own. His sorrow was real, but it was as though it was a sorrow that he needed. He was a man with a direction. He had no time to write to his friends any more, except to send them his verses. He lived at home, with his widowed mother and his sister, and spent his days writing. To Goldberg, when he met him, he simply said: I can never love again. She is my life and always will be.

And then the news came that she was dying. The letter to Sinclair in which she told him this and told him that he was the best thing that had happened in her life, after her son, lay open on his desk for days. It was the last she ever wrote to him. A week later a parcel arrived from her husband, enclosing his letters to her, tied in a bundle, and a jade paperweight which, the note said, she had wanted him to have. And that was all.

Sinclair did not at first seem to understand fully what it was that had happened to him. He went on writing the kind of resigned and Stoic poetry he had recently perfected:

>   Only one Summer grant me, O mighty ones,
>   And but one Autumn leave me for mellow song,
>   So that my heart with its sweet playing
>   Sated more willingly may perish…

>   Most welcome then, O stillness of shades below!
>   Content I shall be, though music of my strings
>   Do not escort me down; for once I
>   Lived as the gods live, and that suffices.

But the mask could not be kept on for long, and another note soon made itself heard, a note of longing for death and oblivion:

> In air may both my love and my grief dissolve!
>   But, through my foolish prayer perhaps, the charm
>   Is breaking; darkness falls and lonely
>   Under the heavens I stand, as always –
>
> Then come, O gentle slumber! The heart desires
>   Too much…

Only his poetry seemed able to act as a bulwark against imminent collapse:

> Be you, O song, my well-disposed refuge, you,
>   That give me joy, be tended with loving care,
>   The garden, where beneath the blossoms
>   Wandering, under the ever-youthful,
>
> I live in safe ingenuousness, when outside
>   With all its breakers distantly mighty Time,
>   The changeful, roars, and the more quiet
>   Sun ever quickens and aids my labour.
>
> You bless benevolently each mortal man's
>   Possessions from above, heavenly potentates,
>   O bless mine also, lest too early
>   Fate put an end to my dream's duration.

But even poetry was not enough. Sinclair set out from his mother's house to visit a friend in Wales. He walked day and night, for three days, his shoes worn to shreds, and collapsing several times on the road. In the mountains he hurried more quickly in his anxiety to get under a friendly roof. He walked in the clouds singing to himself and when he fell he went on singing. The sky seemed very close to the earth and when the rain came he held his face up to it and opened out his arms. It took a while for his friend to recognise him when he eventually knocked at his door, and then, appalled, he and his wife put him straight to bed. But Sinclair got up in the night and went out into the courtyard. The moon shone on the water of the well in the middle of the yard and Wilson and his wife were woken by the sound of someone splashing about in the well. They drew out their friend and put him back to bed, then locked his door and tried to get some sleep themselves.

He grew docile then and would sit in the kitchen with them or follow his friend out into the hills when he went to feed his animals. He spoke very little, and then only to exclaim: How beautiful is the world! Or: Who would have thought the stars were so close! But at times he would grow violent and shout that he had to go to her and was being kept back. His friends would try to calm him as best they could. Wilson would sit for hours by his bed, waiting for him to fall asleep. Then he would creep downstairs, mopping his brow.

He wrote to Sinclair's mother, asking what he should do with him. But she had decided to wash her hands of her son. 'If he cannot find the grace to wish his mother goodbye then I cannot find it in my heart to concern myself with his welfare,' she wrote.

Wilson and his wife were studying her letter when something caught their eye: a shape had flown past the window, falling from the heavens. Outside, Sinclair lay unconscious on the cobbles of the yard.

When he recovered he said he had to leave. Where are you going? they asked. Where have I to go? he said. He left them as he had come, without possessions except the clothes he walked in. But his violence had subsided. He kissed them both and thanked them. I am going to Chester, he said, I am going to my nest.

For the next twenty years he lived in Chester, in a room in the flat of a carpenter, in a tower in the city wall. His mother paid the carpenter a small monthly sum, but the man seemed devoted to his lodger, though no one knew how they had met, or where. His condition deteriorated. The piano on which he used to play grew quite devastated because he so often let off his fury on the instrument. A doctor who examined him at the time reported that 'now he is so far gone that his insanity has developed into raving, and that one can simply no longer understand his speech, which seems to be composed partly of English, partly of Greek and partly of Germanic sounds.' The doctors gave him three years to live. He was left almost without restrictions, treated by the carpenter with kindness and respect, and as a result became calm and regular in his habits and, apart from rare outbreaks of rage and occasional quarrels with the carpenter's apprentices, did not disturb or harm anyone.

He spent much of his time playing the piano, and took up the flute, on which he had been proficient as a young man, and often sang to his own accompaniment. His handwriting, which before the onset of his illness had been soft, very mobile and beautifully formed, gradually became larger, less spontaneous, and was often marred by scrawls and crossings out. It also grew steeper and steeper, as though pressing against an invisible barrier.

The carpenter wrote frequently to his mother. In one letter he said: 'Yesterday I went out again for the first time with your son; he had not left the house since my father took down the apples from the trees. At that time he was outside with us and laughed a great deal when the trees were shaken and the apples fell on his head. On our way home we met Dr Littlechild, who saluted your son and, taking his Homer from his pocket, said: You see, I've brought our old friend. Sinclair looked for a passage in it and gave it to Dr Littlechild to read out, which he did most enthusiastically, which made your son quite delighted, and we then parted, and Littlechild said, Goodbye, Mr Poet, to which your son replied: I know no poets. He seemed pleased with the encounter, though, and laughed a great deal on the way home. However, three days later he broke out and said in his violence: I am no poet, I am librarian to the Duke, and cursed and shouted and could not be calmed for a long time. Now though he is quite calm again.'

The young de Quincey, who was always avid for celebrities, went to see him at about this time. He wrote afterwards: 'An open door showed us a little white-washed room without any of the usual ornaments, in which stood a man who kept his hands in the pockets of his trousers, and who continually bowed to us. The girl, the carpenter's daughter, who had shown me upstairs, whispered: That's him. I approached and asked him how he did. He inclined his head and out of the unintelligible ocean of sounds these words rang out: Your Majesty... Then followed a babble of

French and Greek, and he began to bow and mumble, repeating again and again: Your Royal Highness, Your Royal Highness, this I cannot, must not answer. We were silent. The girl told me to continue speaking to him, but I was at a loss for words. Now he murmured: You must not see my hands. They are dirty. They have been dirtied by my actions. I did not know what to say. He went on: I am just on the point of becoming a Catholic, Your Majesty! I asked him whether the news from Greece pleased him. At this his face lit up, but then grew sombre again and amidst a further stream of incomprehensible words he said again: Your Royal Highness, this I must not, cannot answer! The only intelligible thing he said was to the effect that he had a most pleasant view of the landscape from the window, but then he stood still in the middle of the room and started to bow again and again, without saying anything but: Your Royal Highness... The Royal Gentleman, etc. We could stay no longer and hurried to the carpenter's room.'

De Quincey visited him again, quite frequently. 'His daily habits,' he wrote, 'are most simple. In the morning, especially in summer-time, when he is in every way more agitated and tormented, he rises before or with the sun and leaves the house at once, to walk outside in the garden. This walk usually lasts four or five hours, so that he becomes tired. He likes to divert himself by taking out his handkerchief and hitting the poles of the fence, or by plucking out grass. Whatever he finds, were it no more than a piece of iron or leather, he puts into his pocket and takes home. All the time he speak to himself, asks himself questions and answers them, sometimes with "yes" and sometimes with "no", often with both. He seems to like to say "no".

'Then he enters the house and paces about there. His meals are brought to his room, and he eats with great appetite, likes wine too, and would drink any amount of it if he had the opportunity. When he has finished his meal, he cannot bear to have the plates and cutlery in his room a moment longer, and immediately puts them down outside his door. He insists on having his own property inside his room; everything else is immediately placed in front of the door. The rest of the day passes in soliloquies and in walking about his little room.

'One thing that can keep him occupied for days is his *Atalanta*. A hundred times, as I came to see him, I heard him recite in a loud voice, even before I entered the house. His pathos is great, and *Atalanta* nearly always lies open in his room; he often reads to me out of it. When a passage has become familiar to him, he begins to call out, with violent gesticulation: "O beautiful, beautiful, Your Majesty!" Then he reads on, and suddenly adds: "You see, Your Lordship, a comma, a tiny little comma. But without it the whole world would fall over. It would simply keel right over."'

Sinclair wrote many poems at all periods of his madness, usually straight off for visitors, but he never signed them with his own name. His favourite names for his new self were Giosefini, Turilura, and Buonarotti. De Quincey says: 'He never forgot that I was a writer too and always asked whether I had worked well that day and been industrious. Then he would immediately add: I, sir, no longer possess the same name; I am now called Kilamanjoo. Oui, Your Majesty, you say so, that is your opinion. Oui, Your Majesty, you say so, that is your opinion. No one is harming me.

'I often heard him speak that last phrase,' de Quincey says. 'It seems that he wants to reassure and calm himself that way, by always keeping this thought in his mind: no one is harming me.

'Music has not quite left him,' he goes on. 'He still plays the piano correctly, but in a most extraordinary manner. When he has started playing he continues for days. Then he follows one thought, which is childishly simple, and plays it over many hundreds of times and wears it out to such a degree that it is quite unbearable. To this one must add a quick convulsion or cramp, which sometimes obliges him to pass up and down the keys like lightning, and the unpleasant rattling of his own finger-nails, for he strongly dislikes having them cut, and many tricks are necessary to persuade him, as with stubborn and obstinate children. When he has played for some time, and when his spirit is moved, he suddenly shuts his eyes, raises his head, as if about to languish and pass away, and begins to sing. I could never find out in what language he sang, often as I heard him; but he did so with exuberant pathos, and it made one shudder in every nerve to see and hear him. Melancholy and mournfulness were the moods of his song; one could recognise what had once been a good tenor voice.

'He likes children very much. But they fear him and run away from him. His fear of death is exceptionally great, though indeed he is timorous in every way; the slightest noise convulses him. When he is moved, angry, or only bad-tempered, his whole face twitches, his gestures grow violent, and he screws up his fingers so tightly that one would think there were no joints in them, and sometimes he screams loudly, or quite incoherently addresses long speeches to himself. At such moments one must leave him alone until the storm is abated. When he is quite furious he goes to bed and will not get up for several days.

'One day he suddenly thought of walking to London. His boots were taken away and that enraged him so much that he stayed in bed for two whole weeks. In summer-time unrest often torments him so much that he walks about in the house all night.

'Once,' writes de Quincey, 'I told him I was going to Rome and would not return for a long time; and asked him in jest whether he would be my travelling companion. He smiled as kindly and understandingly as only a wise man can smile, and said: I must stay at home and can no longer travel, gracious sir!

'Sometimes,' de Quincey goes on, 'he gave answers which made one laugh, especially as he gave them with an expression which made one think he was being genuinely ironic. For example, I once asked him how old he was, and he replied with a smile: Seventeen, Your Lordship.'

Another visitor noted: 'One of my acquaintances once addressed him in Italian and asked him whether he had formerly spoken this language: *Si Signore, e la parlo ancora*, was his reply.'   ▌

14. Unterlinden

We arrived in Colmar shortly before lunch. We had stopped in Berne, where I wanted to see the Klees, and, in particular, the 1940 *Wander-Artist*, one of those extraordinary works of Klee's last year, a painting roughly scrawled on notepaper stuck on cardboard, 31 x 29 cm, which shows a figure striding from left to right across a red background, right arm raised in salutation, left arm hanging sadly down to the knee, the face (two black dots in a black circle) turned towards the viewer, the whole enclosed in a roughly painted black frame; then gone on to Basle, where Edith wanted to see the Holbein *Christ in the Tomb*, immortalised by Dostoevsky in *The Idiot*. I decided to spend the day in our hotel room, working on my book. A way had opened up for me in the past few days, when what had seemed intractable suddenly became possible, and seeing the Klee in the flesh, as it were, after having lived with a postcard of it for so long, had made such an impression on me that I wanted to have the day to myself to savour it and work out what it would do to my book.

As I worked, with a growing sense that the end might at last be in sight, I decided to say nothing about it to Edith until we were standing in front of the great Grünewald polyptich in the Unterlinden Museum in Colmar. And the more I thought of the idea the more I liked it. We would stand there, looking at the terrible Crucifixion and talking about it and then I would say, quite casually: You know, the book, I think it's more or less done. Which is why, when she got back to the hotel, exhausted, as one always is by visits to the great museums and art galleries, and asked me how my day had been, I muttered noncommittally, and asked about hers. But I didn't listen to her account. Edith is an enthusiast, but, like many enthusiasts, she does not have the story-telling gift. She runs ahead of herself and then remembers something and runs back and then darts sideways, so that within a few minutes it is impossible to keep up with her. Besides, I was once again going over the steps I had taken that day and the few I knew that still needed to be taken, and marvelling at the clarity and simplicity of it all. There had been times, in the course of the past three years, when I had wondered if I would ever be able to write the book, and even Edith, whose belief in me and my work is far more constant than my own, had, I suspected, herself begun to wonder if perhaps this time I had bitten off more than I could chew. Too often she had turned round in the middle of the night and felt me lying awake and rigid beside her. Are you all right? she would ask. Yes. Are you worrying about the book? Yes. Try to sleep. Yes. But sleep would not come. To me at least it would not come. Poor darling, Edith would murmur, and roll over and at once be lost to the world. The following day, as I struggled, bleary-eyed and hollow-headed, to concentrate on the page in front of me, she would come in with the coffee looking as fresh and carefree as a twelve-year-old. I had no doubt that if I could have slept as she did I would long since have solved the problems posed by the book. But to have slept like that I would not have had to have any problems in the first place.

It was in those circumstances that we had decided to take a holiday on Lake Como, putting the car on the train as far as Milan and then returning in a leisurely way via Berne, Basle, Colmar and Rheims. The thought of seeing the Klees in Berne, and the *Wander-Artist* in particular, and then spending an afternoon in what is perhaps my favourite museum in Europe, the convent of Unterlinden which now houses the Grünewald as well as a host of Rhineland primitives, did more than render the prospect appealing, it made me positively anxious to get started.

Lake Como, which I only knew from photographs and from the opening of *I Promessi Sposi* (I had never got beyond the first hundred pages, enjoyable as I found them), proved to be an inspired choice. Though I was not exactly writing well, I was at least writing. 'Treat every work as if it was your last will and testament', a German writer or philosopher has written (he would, you might say); and if I could not stand by the present work as if it was that, it had at least ceased to be something I was ashamed of and embarrassed by. Every morning I tested it and every morning it at least rang true. In the afternoons we went swimming or for walks round the lake or into the hills; occasionally we went for drives into the surrounding mountains. There were even days when I had to ask Edith to go by herself, when the book called me to return to it in the afternoons, something which had not happened since the start of this particular project. And sometimes, even if I was not at my desk, I felt the need to have the afternoon to myself to wander through at will, free of the obligation of having to talk to another person, even someone as close to me and as under-standing as Edith.

It was in Berne, after seeing the *Wander-Artist*, that I told Edith I would not come to see the Holbein with her when we got to Basle. Although the Berne art gallery, thanks to the generosity of the artist's son, Felix Klee, houses more Klees than any other museum in the world, the *Wander-Artist* is privately owned. I had, after lengthy enquiries, found out the name of the owner, a distant relative of the artist and himself living in Berne, and rung him up from England to see if he would be kind enough to let me have a look at it. Surprisingly, he had not only agreed, but even invited us to dinner. We drove out to his villa, a few miles outside the town. A butler opened the door for us. Herr Haverkampf spoke almost perfect English, which was perhaps not surprising as his wife, a beautiful woman with half-rimmed glasses perched at the end of a delightful little upturned nose, was half American and they had spent several years in Washington and London. After an exquisite dinner, served by the butler and a maid, he showed us round his collection, which consisted mainly of twentieth-century works – Feininger, Schmidt-Rottluf, Soutine, Balthus, even a Schoenberg, Richter, a rough wooden Baselitz sculpture, Freud, Kossoff, de Stael, and a considerable number of Klees. The *Wander-Artist*, however, stood out. We looked at it for a long time. Like so many of the paintings Klee did in his last year it exuded a sense of desperate urgency yet remained curiously aloof, inhab-iting its own still world. Is he waving airily to us as he passes by or raising his hand in warning? Is it melancholy or indifference that is to be read into his expression? Is he the smiling Pentheus or the despairing Agave? Klee knew better than anyone how to give and withhold at the same time, and the *Wander-Artist* is the supreme example of his art.

I have made many gifts to the Klee-archive here in Berne, Georg Haverkampf said, but this I could not give. Each time my conscience urged me to make it available to the general public my selfishness rose up and repressed it. He laughed with that throaty laugh peculiar to the German Swiss. It is generous of you to let admirers come into your house to see it, I said. It is admiration that unites us, he said. I take almost as much pleasure in entertaining those who have made the pilgrimage to see the work as I do in the work itself.

Afterwards, in the living-room, Leila Haverkampf tried to engage me in conversation, pushing her strange little glasses continuously back up her nose and in the same gesture pulling back the hair from her face, and I tried to be as civil as possible, but it was difficult: my thoughts were all with the painting we had just seen. Georg Haverkampf seemed to be much taken with Edith, who was describing the walks we had taken round Lake Como. Let me show you something, Mrs Haverkampf said, laying a surprisingly firm hand on my arm. I followed her upstairs. Art is all very well, she said, leading me through a part of the house I had not previously seen, but this is something else again. She opened a French window and we stepped out onto a terrace. There was a full moon and the mountains rising up around us were plainly visible, but seen as though through a gauze mesh. We stood there looking up at them for a while. Nature does not move you? Mrs Haverkampf asked. Her question made me uncomfortable. I could feel her looking at me in the moonlight, pushing her glasses back up her nose, her blonde hair falling over her eyes. Of course it does, I said foolishly. She put a hand on my wrist and the warmth flooded through the thin fabric of my suit and shirt sleeve and seemed to run right into my arm. You don't have to say that, she said. I looked at my watch. I think we ought to be getting back, I said. We have to set out early tomorrow. Of course you do, she said. But you have our number. I hope you will visit us again. She led me back to the living-room. Herr Haverkampf was laughing throatily at something Edith had said. My wife has shown you the views? he asked as we came in. Remarkable, I said. When the moon is full it is remarkable, he said. And when there is no moon it is remarkable as well. The stars shine very brightly here upon us in the Bernese Alps.

We took our leave. What a fascinating woman, Edith said as soon as we got into the car. Why? I asked. You didn't think so? I found her glasses rather ridiculous, I said. I suppose they were, she said. We drove in silence through the moonlight, and it was then I told her I would not be coming with her to see the Holbein. I knew she would be disappointed. We all like to share our passions with those we love, but she knew me better than to make a fuss. And when, the following afternoon, she started to tell me about her day, about the effect on her of that extraordinary painting, two metres long and only twenty centimetres high, which shows a gaunt bearded man lying in a coffin, the contemplation of which, said Dostoevsky in a letter, made him lose his faith, a sentiment he puts into the mouth of Prince Myshkin in *The Idiot,* I tried to show an interest, but my mind was with my book. While she was talking to me – she had moved on to a description of the Tinguely installation, *The Band* – I was imagining what it would feel like to arrive at the end of my book at last and turn and look back over the long road I had travelled.

On the drive from Basle to Colmar we talked about the Hölderlin poems we had been reading together. I asked her how she understood the opening lines of the second version of that late poem, *Mnemosyne,* supposedly written in the poet's madness:

> Ein Zeichen sind wir, deutungslos
> Schmerzlos sind wir und haben fast
> Die Sprache in der Fremde verloren.

> (A sign we are, without interpretation
> Without pain we are and have almost
> Lost our language in foreign parts.)

Did she understand that *Schmerzlos* in a positive or a negative

sense? And if it was positive, did that then make the first line positive? How could it be positive, she said, given the second limb of
the sentence? Surely to lose our language and to lose it *in der
Fremde,* abroad, was the worst thing that could happen to
anyone? But what, I said, if our language was the cause of all our
trouble? What if we needed to lose it in order to find ourselves
again? The implication is surely, Edith said, that once we were
interpretable signs, once we had a language of our own, and if it
caused us pain that pain was what made us human and that pain
was bearable because it had a meaning. I grant you that to be
without pain is in a sense a sign of no longer being alive, I said,
but perhaps we have to recognise and accept that that is our
condition, and then we may be able to live.

We were still arguing about it when we arrived in Colmar and
parked the car. As we had been talking I had been wondering
where would be the best place to tell Edith my secret: should it be
on the balcony overlooking the hall in which the great polyptych
is housed, or should it be as we stood in front of the Crucifixion?
I wanted to make the most of that moment, but as we entered the
museum I had still not made up my mind what would be the most
suitable spot.

I had not remembered that the place was so popular. The
entrance was teeming with parties of schoolchildren and
coachloads of tourists, German, Dutch, French, even Polish and
Russian. But then there are tourists everywhere these days, they
even penetrate as far as Twickenham and Pinner. It is as if the
whole world is on the move, eager to gaze upon anything that is
not its habitual home: the Japanese come with their cameras to
Pinner and the inhabitants of Pinner go with their cameras to Bali;
the Balinese flock to Paris and the Parisians – well, the Parisians
are the exception that proves the rule, for they only go as far as
their holiday homes in the Cevennes.

The Unterlinden Museum not only houses some of the greatest
paintings in the world, it is itself a lovely, peaceful building, with
its cloisters and fountain, its stone floors and wooden beams. For
the first time in a long while – perhaps since I had started the book
– I felt at peace with the world. I let scenes from the book float
through my mind, and found that the image of Leila Haverkampf

looking at me in the moonlight through her funny glasses seemed to have settled into many of them, as though she too had been brought into being by my imagination and my work on the book. We strolled through the first rooms, the Rhineland primitives exuding a strong sense of trust in the world, their dark pictures glowing. Edith turned aside into a small room I had not remembered and stopped in front of a strange still-life. Utterly different from anything else in the museum, it was at once self-contained and utterly mysterious. Divided horizontally into two parts, it showed a shallow cupboard, the top half consisting of two doors, one of which was partly open in *trompe-l'oeil*, the lower half consisting of a shelf on which stood a number of containers, while more – bottles, flasks and the like – hung from nails set in the wall.

We stood in front of it for some time. I was surprised by it but was not really taking it in, was already in the big gallery with the Grünewald, and had indeed turned to move on, when Edith took my arm. What? I asked, surprised at the gesture, which was unlike her. I want to talk to you, she said. Something in her voice made me stop and look at her. But she was staring straight ahead at the still life. What about? I said. Us, she said. Us? What about us? We were alone in that little room and suddenly the Grünewald seemed very far away. Have you thought about us? she said. What do you mean thought? I said. Well I have, she said. I've thought a great deal about us in the past few weeks, and yesterday in Basle I came to a decision. Decision? I said. What are you talking about? I can't go on, she said. What do you mean? I said. I can't go on, she repeated. I'm going to take the train back. You don't like to drive? I said. You haven't understood, she said. I can't go on. I've had enough. Edith, I said, are you saying you want to leave me? Yes, she said. Look, I said, what is this? Can we sit down somewhere and talk? No, she said. What's happened? I said. Can you explain? No, she said. You can't or you won't? Both, she said. I couldn't believe this was happening. Edith, I said, we have been together half our lives. We have two children. We are happy. We are going to die together. No we're not, she said. Do you know what you're saying? I said. Yes, she said. We have two children, I said again. We're happily married. You can't do this to us. Our children are both married, she said. They have nothing to do with it. Is there someone else? I asked her, and the thought even crossed my mind that Georg Haverkampf was perhaps lurking in the next room and would appear at a signal from her to confront me. I burst out laughing. You find it funny? she said. Is there someone else? I asked again. No, she said, I'm afraid not. Why afraid? I said. Because that you might understand, she said. I thought about it. Yes, I said, I suppose I might. But I said it more to go along with her than from any conviction of my own. The thought of Edith leaving me for another man, or rather, of another man being ready to go off with her, was one I found it impossible to imagine. I'm going to get my suitcase out of the car and take a taxi to the station, she said. Is this a joke? I said. Goodbye, she said. You aren't going to explain? I said. No, she said. I don't feel I have anything to explain.

We stood for a while longer in front of that still life. Well, she said, goodbye, Gerald. She turned and walked away. I went on staring at the picture. After a while I looked around, in the vague hope perhaps that she had stopped at the door, but she hadn't. ▌

15. Mrs Goldberg

When you are absent I take to my notebook. It is the only way I know of being with you. It has always been like that. Martha will always be scribbling, Papa used to say. I cannot remember when I discovered the comfort that writing brings. Why should it be so? Nobody will read it, not even myself. Yet writing things down, bending over the white page, dipping the pen in the ink, pausing, looking up, starting again – all that brings release and appeasement, such as merely closing the eyes and imagining never does. Mama is gone today, I remember writing down, she will not return for at least a week. Papa died yesterday in his sleep, I wrote later. I held his hand before but I am not sure he knew it was me.

Why do we feel the need to write down this sort of thing? It explains nothing. It does not alter the facts. It tells us nothing we did not already know. And yet it brings relief. Of that there can be no doubt. The feeling is palpable. As one writes the pain round the heart eases, the knots inside one are loosed, the state of shock into which one had been thrown gives way to something else, one picks up ones normal rhythm of breathing again, of moving. Not for long, of course. There is no telling when the world will strike again. But the release is genuine for all that. It is as though the blow had altered one's relation to time, to one's own body, so that it is as if one were perpetually falling into a black hole but never quite being engulfed, as if one were perpetually starting and then stopping and then starting again, so that one cannot eat or sleep or walk or think or indeed do anything to any purpose, yet one is not exhausted enough to sleep or even rest, but must be perpetually starting again and picking up something to do and then at once laying it by. But writing down the simple facts seems to act as a release, as if one had at last come to accept what before one had refused to acknowledge. It seems, for a while at least, to set one on a road upon which it is good to walk and at the end of which one is rewarded with genuine tiredness. But why does writing do that to one when thinking cannot? What is the secret balm that lies in the simple act of putting words down on paper as I am doing now?

I have never told him. Not that he would laugh. He would understand at once. Perhaps he knows and does. It is of no significance. I did not tell Papa or any of my sisters, though in that house nothing could be hidden for long. And I did not *try* to hide. I simply did not like to be observed. It is like crying. Something it is good to do from time to time but which one wishes to do alone. There is nothing more painful than to be seen crying. Either observed in silence or else comforted by those who do not and cannot understand. And when they think they do it is even worse.

I suppose it is because one feels so naked, so vulnerable. That is easy to understand where crying is concerned, but what of writing? If I were writing a letter I would not mind being observed. Or doing the accounts. And if what I am writing is so secret that I want no one to read it, that does not alter the fact that my appearance will be no different from what it would be if I were writing a letter. To others, that is. But I know that from the inside it feels wholly different. And perhaps that is why writing brings release, because one is both vulnerable and, in a curious way, active and in control. That is why writing is so much better than crying. And often, of course, as now, it is hardly like it at all. I do not really grieve at your absence. I merely miss your presence. I have enough to do, even now that the children are all grown, bar one. But if I did not confide these thoughts to my notebook I would miss you even more. I would range through the house, I know, putting order where it would not be necessary, and then in bed I would lie awake, feeling confusedly that things still needed to be done, that I had forgotten to take the bread out of the oven or to clean one of the shelves in the pantry.

I had never thought of any of this till I sat down half an hour ago filled with the need to write about you. That is what writing is like. The sheet of paper before one and the pen in one's hand seem to allow those things to emerge which one knew but didn't know one knew. It may not be very interesting or very profound, but it brings relief. Like hugging you. But why is it not sufficient to sit in my chair and imagine myself hugging you? After all, when I write here in my notebook you are no more present than if I closed my eyes and thought of you. Indeed, less so perhaps, since if I close my eyes I can see you, whereas when I write I certainly do not. But then when I hug you I do not see you, I feel you. And that is what seems to happen with writing. But why should that be so? To feel you, you have to be present and close to me, and now you are neither. Yet I am sure this is the truth, that when I close my eyes I see you but when I write I feel you.

But how can one feel what is not present? How can one touch that which is absent? Because by feel I do not mean touch, for hugging would not be hugging if one did not touch the other.

These matters are too difficult for me. I know I am right but I do not have the mind to understand why I am right. Perhaps now I have thought of it the explanation will reveal itself to me later. I have known that to happen with other things. But it does not matter. It does not matter at all if I never understand the *how*, for I am sure I am right and that there is a close affinity between the feeling I get from hugging you and the feeling I get from writing to you.

Vive la différence! you always say. You tall, me short, you thin, me plump, you a Jew and me so English I had never thought of difference till I met you. The cardinal sin is to abolish difference, you said to me when I first expressed sorrow at the fact that there were so many differences between us. What would the world be like if all the flowers were but one flower, all trees but one tree, all the mountains levelled and all the valleys filled in? It would be a nightmare, you said, and I had to agree with you. Yet in spite of that human beings long for sameness, you said. We are terrified of that which is different from ourselves and from what we already know. This fear is the bane of life, you said. Look at what happened to Spinoza. The Jews hated him for being different, for speaking in ways they only dimly understood. So what did they do? They cast him out. As though that would make everything all right again, as if once they had cast him out it would be as though he had never been and they could go on as they had always done. But mark the irony, you said. What made Spinoza different was that he preached that we are all at bottom the same and that is a crazy and dangerous doctrine which they were right to fear and distrust. He did so of course from the best of motives, but that does not stop him being wrong. They sensed the value of difference and cast him out for denying that. What a crazy twisted thing is the human heart and human history! He saw the difference as prejudice and they proved that he was right even as they told him that he was wrong. We need to be proud of difference, you said, we need to affirm difference, but to fight prejudice wherever we find it. Are you not contradicting yourself? Annabel asked him. Is not logic against you? Logic perhaps, you said, but not the human heart. But why should you trust the human heart, she pressed him, rather than the laws of your country or your religion? She was the clever one, Papa called her Portia to tease her. Danny is like her. He is always laying traps for his father and seems to feel that to argue with him proves his independence. Yet their arguments always seem to end in laughter rather than in tears. Not so with Annabel. Her nose would grow white when she was not satisfied with an answer or thought her arguments were being evaded. The human heart, you said, can only mislead if we do not pay sufficient attention to it. But logic constantly misleads because it constantly simplifies what is complex. If you invoke the human heart whenever logic is against you, she said, then how is argument possible? I merely pointed out, you said, that prejudice and difference are not at all the same thing. What then should the Jews have done with Spinoza? she said. Should they have welcomed what he said or made clear the nature of the difference between them? I hold no brief for the Jews of Amsterdam, you said, or for the philosopher. I merely point out the irony of the whole situation. He wishes to abolish difference, which he sees as being like a piece of grit which blocks the smooth functioning of the mechanism of the clock, and they eject him from their midst because to them he is like a piece of grit which blocks the smooth functioning of their system. Irony is no answer, she said, nor is it possible simply to point it out and not come down on the one side or the other. If it were to impinge directly on my life, you said, then of course I would have to take a decision. But as it does not any decision I would take would be meaningless. Not so, she said, and the argument went on till late into the evening.

With Danny the arguments are very different. He is as sure of himself as Annabel but has your ability to let things be if no agreement seems possible. And he is as ready to laugh as you are, and as ready to shift his ground if an impasse is reached. And, like you, he is always keen to argue not about abstract ideas but about specific details, such as the kind of mathematical formula needed to describe the shape of a sea shell or the prosody of a line of poetry. God is in the details, you always say and God is a maker, let us learn how to make from a study of God's own makings and from the works of those he has seen fit to inspire with his own breath. When my mind is blank and my spirits low, you have often said to me, then contact with nature or with a great work of art takes me out of myself and my petty troubles and gives me back the sense of how much there is to learn and to observe and how little is the time we are vouchsafed here on earth in which to do so. Danny takes after you in that as in so much else, though there is something a little dry, a little cold, in his analysis of works of literature, a barely concealed desire to emulate and impress you and even perhaps to overcome you and force you to admit defeat. Such as the time when, in reading the *Odyssey* and coming to the passage where the disguised Odysseus recounts to Penelope that he has seen Odysseus and welcomed him as a guest in his home in Crete, he pointed to the contiguity of the words *Odysseus* and *I* in the line: 'There Odysseus I saw and gifts to him gave', suggesting that for a moment the reader or listener imagines the disguise is about to drop and Odysseus to reveal himself. When you pointed out that this was far-fetched he triumphantly showed that in that line in the Greek, *Oduseia* and *ego* were followed by the caesura, and that this was an extremely rare example of such a thing, there being only about eight examples, he said, of such an 'illicit' hiatus in the whole of the *Iliad* and *Odyssey*. The implication was thus that one would have to pause after *ego* and the line would momentarily read 'And there I, Odysseus', before concluding 'saw and gave guest gifts to'. Even you had to admit that he had a point there.

Before you left you brought me a daffodil from the garden. It is here in a vase before me now. Perhaps I will try to draw it when I have finished writing, though drawing never satisfied me the way writing does. Perhaps because I am so bad at it. All five of us were taught to draw. Mary was the best, though Anthea was the most careful and meticulous. To learn to draw is to learn to see, Papa always said. Perhaps to learn to write is to learn to feel? I am not sure about that. Besides, one does not have to learn to write in the way one has to learn to draw. Writing is a kind of silent speaking. Or a speaking which does not immediately vanish away. All those who can speak and know how to form letters can write, but what are the equivalents of letters in drawing? The object does not have to be beautiful in itself, Papa said. It need not be a flower or a sunset. One can do a beautiful drawing of a stone and an ugly drawing of a flower, he said, a beautiful drawing of a hunchback and an ugly drawing of a lovely woman. I held his hand as he lay dying. Why could I not be given the chance to do the same for little Benjamin?

Let it be. Let it be. I have thought of that enough and there is no answer. Let it be.

You will write to me, I know. And soon you will be back. But I have grown used to your presence in the house and it is hard to be alone. Though I am not alone, strictly speaking. Sarah sleeps upstairs and the dog is at my feet. The cats sleep on the hearth before the fire, wrapped in each other's arms, as always. When I extinguish the light and go upstairs to bed they will wait a while and when the fire dies down and the house starts to grow cold they will come running up the stairs and jump onto my bed and burrow down under the blankets, purring loudly and thinking nothing of waking me in the process. When you are not there, I must admit, it is a comfort to have them close to me.

Are you at the moment reading to Mr Westfield? Does he lie in his great bed and snore? You read so beautifully, with such controlled passion. It is as if the book itself were speaking when you read, you yourself seem to vanish and only the book survives. And you taught all of us to read aloud. Or rather, you did not teach but, by making us all do it, showed us how much pleasure it could give us. To read and to sing and to play music. Every family should play music together, you said, and you made sure all the children held instruments almost before they could walk. In music, you said, all the voices are different and all the voices are equal. No voice tries to silence any of the others and no one should raise his voice above any of the others, but rather listen to the others and add his voice to the rest. Miss Pettigrew, you said. Mr Goldberg, I said. And we both laughed. It was the first time I did not flinch at the sound of my name, because it was in your mouth. I knew why you had come as if we had rehearsed the scene many times. Mrs Goldberg? you asked, and I said, Oh yes, please, and we both laughed again, and that was that. That was the first time you read to me. You read me Shakespeare's 'The Phoenix and the Turtle'. I can hear it yet:

So they loved as love in twain
Had the essence but in one,
Two distincts, division none,
Number there in love was slain.

Hearts remote, yet not asunder;
Distance and no space was seen,
Twixt this Turtle and his Queene;
But in them it were a wonder.

So between them Love did shine,
That the Turtle saw his right,
Flaming in the Phoenix sight;
Either was the others mine.

Property was thus appalled,
That the self was not the same:
Single Natures double name,
Neither two nor one was called.

Reason in itself confounded,
Saw Division grow together,
To themselves yet either neither,
Simples were so well compounded.

That it cried, how true a twain,
Seemeth this concordant one,
Love hath Reason, Reason none,
If what parts, can so remain.

If what parts can so remain. Yes. If what parts can so remain.
And has so remained ever since, through birth and death and
separation and leaking roofs and not enough money to pay for the
man to mend it and your headaches and my colds. Saw Division
grow together. Yet never merging into one. *Vive la différence!* How
I love you, Mr Goldberg!

16. The Challenge

Several years earlier Goldberg had faced his greatest challenge. His son, who was one of several poets in the pay of the King, had let it be known that a visit from his father to the court would not come amiss. Goldberg had resisted for as long as he could, claiming that he was too old to take part in the flytings or poetic competitions in which he knew the King delighted. Eventually, however, he realised that he would have to give way.

The news quickly spread through the King's entourage that 'old Goldberg has come', and, flanked by his son and Sir Geoffrey Newbold, the Master of the King's Chamber, he was ushered into the royal presence.

– Woher seid Ihr? the King asked in a low voice as soon as Goldberg had stopped in front of the deep red armchair in which the King was lounging.

– Aus Mannheim, Eure Majestät.

– Ah, Mannheim. Reist Ihr oft dorthin?

– Jetzt nicht mehr, Eure Majestät. Ich habe nunmehr dieses Land zu meiner Heimat gemacht.

– Sehr gut. Ein Mensch kann nur an einem Orte wirklich zu Hause sein. Es ist nicht möglich, an zwei Orten zugleich zu leben. Und nun sollten wir, um der Anderen willen, unsere Konversation auf Englisch weiterführen.

– Gewiss, Eure Majestät.

– I have read many of your works, Mr Goldberg, said the King, raising his voice.

– I am most gratified, Your Majesty, said Goldberg, following suit.

– I have to confess, the King continued, that I understood not a word.

Goldberg was silent.

– However, the King went on, I am assured that what you write is very good. Very good indeed.

Goldberg bowed his head and waited.

– Will you improvise something for us? the King went on.

– I will do what I can, Your Majesty.

– I have a topic here, the King said, tugging at his waistcoat pocket and producing a crumpled piece of paper. He felt about on the little table beside his chair for his glasses and put them on his nose. Smoothing the sheet of paper out on his knees, he peered at it. A little topic, he said, which I thought might amuse you.

Goldberg waited, head bowed.

– A man who had enough wanted everything, said the King. As a result he was left with nothing. Treat this not as a morality but as a tragedy.

Goldberg smiled.

– You may begin, the King said.

Goldberg closed his eyes. Everybody waited.

After a while Goldberg opened his eyes again. He smiled at the King and looked round the room.

– In one of his most beautiful poems, he began, John Donne wrote as follows:

'Tis the year's midnight, and it is the day's,
Lucy's, who scarce seven hours herself unmasks,
   The sun is spent, and now his flasks
   Send forth light squibs, no constant rays;
     The world's whole sap is sunk:
The general balm th'hydroptic earth has drunk,
Whither, as to the bed's feet, life is shrunk,
Dead and interred; yet all these seem to laugh,
Compared with me, who am their epitaph.

The poem, said Goldberg, is entitled 'A Nocturnal Upon S. Lucy's Day, being the shortest day'. St Lucy's Day, 13 December, was indeed the shortest day under the unreformed Julian calendar, the winter solstice, when the sun entered the sign of the goat. The name Lucy itself of course betokens light, and in Donne's life we know of at least two Lucys, his patroness, Lucy, Countess of Bedford, and his daughter, both of whom, strangely, died in the same year, 1627. The poem, though, probably refers to Donne's beloved wife, Ann, who died in 1617. The term 'nocturnal' is not, as far as I have been able to find out, used by any other English poet as the description of a type of poem, though it sounds as though it should be, like 'elegy' or 'sonnet'. What the poet has done here is to indicate the supposed time of writing, or the supposed subject of the poem, night, and to suggest that this is a poetic form, that he has written a 'nocturne'.

– The first stanza, continued Goldberg, which this is, appears, until the last line, to restrict itself to a description of this, the shortest day of the year. But it does so with such a strange mixture of the subjective and the scientific as to leave us feeling that the year and indeed the universe is in reality a huge beast whose hour has now come. 'The year's whole sap is sunk ... as to the bed's feet, life is shrunk, dead and interred.' No one but Donne, Goldberg went on, noting that the King had closed his eyes and was lying back in his deep red chair as though himself sunk in sleep, no one but Donne would have thought of such a comparison, and no one but Donne would have had the daring to compare the apparent death of the entire world to the feet of a bed, but, as always with this strangest and most haunting of poets, once we have been presented with the image we can never forget it.

– I want, said Goldberg, to focus on this image for a little while longer. When we read the line, 'Whither, as to the bed's feet, life is shrunk', do we see the feet of a particular bed in our mind's eye? I do not think so. Neither a particular bed nor a generalised one. The image works, he said, not because it presents us with a stark visual image but because the associations of the word 'bed' and of the word 'feet', thus brought together combine to convey a particular feeling. 'Bed' by itself could suggest laziness, or voluptuousness, or sickness. Combined with the word 'feet' only the last of these associations is activated. Together they convey a sense of a person stretched or laid out on a bed, in death perhaps (since we have 'dead and interred' in the very next line), with his or her feet sticking out at the end of the bed. Curiously then what by the cold light of logic might have seemed absurd or at least inept as an image, takes on the powerful connotations of the end of life, life seen as a body lying in death upon a bed.

– And yet, went on Goldberg, Donne ends this first stanza by asserting that even this state of total extinction is joyful in comparison with his own, 'who am their epitaph'. He is, he claims, merely writing on the tombstone of the extinguished world, twice removed from life.

– With this, continued Goldberg, noting that the King's courtiers at least, his son amongst them, were apparently paying attention, with this Donne moves into his second stanza:

> Study me then, you who shall lovers be
> At the next world, that is, at the next spring:
>   For I am every dead thing
>   In whom love wrought new alchemy.
>   For his love did express
> A quintessence even from nothingness,
> From dull privations, and lean emptiness
> He ruined me, and I am re-begot
> Of absence, darkness, death; things which are not.

– With this stanza, continued Goldberg, a surprising new element is introduced: love. Love is the opposite of death and extinction, of the utter hopelessness of the first stanza. But of course it is not introduced as a contrast at all. Love will flourish again 'at the next world', which is only the next Spring but the hope of love for him is only a mirage. He himself is 'every dead thing/In whom love wrought new alchemy', but this is a strange sort of alchemy, one that resurrects him not as a living being but 're-begot of absence, darkness, death: things which are not'.

– It seems then that, had he not loved so much he would not now find himself this 'lean emptiness'. For, he goes on,

> All others, from all things, draw all that's good,
> Life, soul, form, spirit, whence they being have;

I, by love's limbeck, am the grave
Of all, that's nothing.

How is that? He explains:

                    Oft a flood
    Have we too wept, and so
 Drowned the whole world, us too: oft did we grow
To be two chaoses, when we did show
Care to aught else; and often absences
Withdrew our souls, and made us carcases.

But I am by her death (which word wrongs her)
Of the first nothing, the elixir grown;
    Were I a man, that I were one,
    I needs must know; I should prefer
        If I were any beast,
Some ends, some means, yea plants, yea stones detest,
And love; all, all some properties invest;
If I an ordinary nothing were,
As shadow, a light, and body must be here.

It is his love, his extraordinary, his exclusive love, which has led
to this. Had he not loved he would not now be in this position;
had he been content to be an ordinary mortal, an 'ordinary
nothing', as he puts it, he would not still be present, a body,
casting shadow, filled with light. But his love and hers, which gave
him the whole world, their tears drowning everything but themselves, has now, with her death, taken the world and more than
the world from him:

But I am none; nor will my sun renew.
You lovers, for whose sake, the lesser sun
    At this time to the Goat is run
    To fetch new lust, and give it you.
        Enjoy your summer all;
Since she enjoys her long night's festival,
Let me prepare towards her, and let me call

This hour her vigil, and her eve, since this
Both the year's, and the day's deep midnight is.

– For normal lovers, went on Goldberg, seeing that the King
was now awake and listening, this darkest day of the year is also
a time of retrenchment and renewal, a time when the sun itself
has gone into the goat to stoke up its fires as ordinary lovers
prepare in darkest winter for their summer. But now for him
there is only the knowledge that his Lucy, his light, is actually
enjoying the night, making of it her festival, so that all that is left
for him to do is to prepare to join her and to accept that from this
midnight no dawn will follow. He is lost to himself as he has lost
the world. Wanting everything, he is left with nothing. That is his
tragedy.

Goldberg stopped. Everyone waited for the King. He took his
time, then brought his hands together in quiet applause. At once
his courtiers did likewise.

– I see, said the King, that I was not misled.

Goldberg waited, head bowed.

– You have done well, said the King.

– Thank you, Your Majesty, said Goldberg.

On the way out his son, who was accompanying him, said:

– I have a confession to make.

– How so?

– A part of me hoped you would fail.

– That is natural, said Goldberg.

– Natural?

– Of course.

– You do not condemn me?

– I congratulate you on your honesty. I would have expected no
less, though, from my son.

– Do not forget, he added, as the doors were opened before
them, that a part of you also wished me to succeed.

– Yes, his son said, that is true too.

*

Ten days later a parcel arrived for the King. It contained a letter from Goldberg and a number of separate manuscripts, tied together.

'Your Majesty,' the letter began, 'it was with great sorrow that I returned here immediately upon leaving Your presence. Sorrow because I was all too conscious of the fact that I had not carried out the task you set me to my complete satisfaction, even if to the best of my ability, and sorrow that I had failed to give Your Majesty the pleasure you expected and deserved. I have no excuses except the coming on of age and a consequent loss of the spirit of invention, especially when I am called upon to improvise, something I recall being able to do without second thought in earlier days. Even as I was speaking I was aware of the fact that my choice of subject was not of the best, being perhaps too heavy and ponderous for the occasion, when something lighter and more immediately appealing might have been better. But I had made my choice and could only stay with it. Upon returning here, though, I immediately set myself to analyse the reasons for my dissatisfaction and to see whether there was any way to put it right.

'Let me begin by saying that I quickly found my analysis of the poem by John Donne to be deeply flawed. I used it, Your Majesty will recall, as an example of someone who, having enough, wanted everything, and as a result was left with nothing, as your Majesty had bidden me. But is this indeed how the poem should be read? Did the speaker have "enough" before he fell in love? Nothing tells us so, and the whole of experience teaches us that a life of celibacy is not and never can be enough. Did he want "everything"? Again, the answer has to be no. If his Lucy became everything to him, that was not because he wanted it – he merely wished to marry her. And, finally, did he in fact, as a result of his love, eventually lose all he had? A closer reading of the poem suggests not, I believe.

'The speaker describes himself as "re-begot/ Of absence, darkness, death; things which are not". Others, he says, "from all things draw all that's good", while "I, by love's limbeck, am the grave of all, that's nothing". He insists that by her death he is "Of the first nothing, the elixir grown". Even stones, he asserts, detest and love, only he is so much a nothing that he can feel nothing.

He only knows that there will be no renewal for him in the Spring as there is for the rest of the world. And yet – and this, since it comes at the climax of the poem, seems to me to hold its secret – and yet she, the lost one, the light lost in darkness, Lucy, is not exactly nothing. "Since she enjoys her long night's festival", he concludes,

> Let me prepare towards her, and let me call
> This hour her vigil, and her eve, since this
> Both the year's and the day's deep midnight is.

'It is true, Your Majesty, that the word "enjoys" did not have in Donne's day the exact meaning it has for us today. In many cases it simply meant "experiences". Nonetheless, for Donne to employ this word at this precise juncture suggests – and the rest of the line bears that out – that Lucy is somehow triumphant in her "long night's festival". She has transformed the darkness into some-thing positive, not by changing it to light, but by somehow imbuing negativity itself with a powerful life. Thus the speaker's "Let me prepare towards her" suggests a total reorientation of his being, as he gets ready to alter his most profound perceptions and to find in "absence, darkness, death; things which are not" the true centre of his affective being. It is a *volte face* as powerful and decisive as that experienced by Dante when, at the end of his *Inferno*, he follows Virgil down the hairy legs of Satan and, emerging on the other side, looks back and sees Satan, stuck head down in the earth, thus understanding that all that had seemed upright in the world he has just left is really upside-down, and all that had seemed upside-down is really the right way up. In Donne's poem too the speaker-poet at the end, far from having "lost everything" has only lost the world, which is now seen to be itself the true nothing, and is on the way to gaining all. By the alchemy of his poetry he has made us read the last lines not as tragedy but as, in Dante's sense, a comedy, something that will end well, and made of the terms "deep midnight" something that glows for us with a hidden and splendid light:

> Since she enjoys her long night's festival,
> Let me prepare towards her, and let me call

This hour her vigil and her eve, since this
Both the year's and the day's deep midnight is.

'Your Majesty, having analysed the poem and shown that my improvised commentary upon it was deeply flawed, allow me now to present you with the result of more pondered labours.

'Let me begin by offering you a variation on the theme proposed, viz.

'Once upon a time there was a man whose name has been expunged from the annals of the world. When he was twenty a wonderful thing happened to him. He came in contact with a man who promised to transform the dull world in which he had grown up into the perfect paradise. Let he who would find his life lose it, this man said, let him abandon his father and his mother, his brothers and his sisters, and follow me. He became this man's most fervent disciple, the most ardent believer in his message of all those who followed him. The world you live in is a dead world, this man proclaimed, and you who live in it are dead though you think yourselves alive. Follow me and you will find the waters of true life, follow me and you will be born again. Many listened to this man's message, and many were won over, but our man was the most ardent disciple. The leader swept all before him and, with our man and eleven other close followers, he travelled the length and breadth of the country, preaching his message of life and renewal.

'The authorities grew alarmed. If this man was to be allowed to seduce the entire country with his promises, what would happen to civil society? At best a wave of unrest would sweep the country, at worst a revolution would ensue, with consequences no one could foresee. What was needed was to find evidence of civil subversion against this man and to get rid of him legally and with the least possible fuss.

'The leader's rhetoric changed. He explained to his disciples that his death was imminent, but also that it was the final act in a cosmic drama that had been unfolding since the beginning of time. With his death God's plan for mankind would finally be revealed and those who believed in him would be led into eternal life.

'It had all been written in the Scriptures, he explained. He would be betrayed by one of his own disciples and handed over to the authorities. He would be crucified, die and be buried. And then on the third day he would rise again and the hour of the victory of the forces of light would have come at last.

'But who would perform the act of betrayal? Who loved him so much that he would be prepared to sacrifice not just his reputation but his eternal soul for the sake of the final victory? Our man did not hesitate. History has it that he sold his master for thirty pieces of silver. He knew better. He and he alone was the instrument whereby mankind as a whole would be redeemed. The master was only to die in the flesh, but the one who betrayed him would die in the spirit. The master was secure in the knowledge that after death he would rise again and lead mankind into paradise. One man, though, would be missing. Yet that man was the most important, the one whose sacrifice had made all else possible. Our man had no hesitation. He 'betrayed' his master.

'Later, unable to live with the thought that he and he alone would suffer the torments of eternal damnation, he hanged himself. Of course there had been no need of his absurd sacrifice. If it was decreed that the master would die in order to be born again, then that would happen. Our man, imagining in his pride that the destiny of the universe lay in his hands, lost everything. His whole life was revealed as having been driven by the desire to give up what merely sufficed in order to gain everything, with the result that he was left with nothing; no longer believing in the value of his supreme act of sacrifice, driven by thoughts of eternal damnation, scorned by those he had betrayed and by those to whom he had betrayed them, he died a figure of horror and pity to the world.

'Who was this man? Nobody knows, for, as I have said, his name has been expunged from the annals of the world. But, some time later, the scribes who set about recording the life of the master, feeling that greater verisimilitude would be achieved by giving the object of loathing a name, and convinced that the Jews, of whom their master had of course been one, had been his greatest enemies and betrayers, lighted upon the name of Judas, and so he has been known ever since.'

With the parcel containing this narrative were two other manuscripts. The first consisted of seven tiny tales, each a variation on the theme, and each preceded by a Roman numeral:

'1. A young man leaves his family and home in order to pursue a dream of glory and fulfilment. He returns, many years later, wealthy beyond the imagining of those he had left behind, marries, and lives out the remainder of his life in his home town, admired and respected, with a loving wife and children who are a success in every way. On his death bed he thinks: So this was life? At least if I had stayed at home I could have ended up dreaming that, if only I had had the courage to seek my fortune instead of remaining at home, I would have ended up a happy man.

'2. The man condemned to exile for daring to voice his criticism of his government in public accepted his fate willingly. History, he knew, would vindicate him. One day a message reached him, telling him that the regime which had exiled him had been overthrown and inviting him to return to head his country. One glance at it, however, was enough to convince him that it was a hoax.

'3. The youngest and plainest of three sisters grew up into a beauty and married a prince. But her meanness made their lives a misery. When her husband admonished her she said: It's not my fault. I was deprived of so much when I was young that even now that I have everything I want I am always afraid that it will be taken from me. Her husband said: When you had nothing you expected no more. Now you have everything you are perpetually discontented. You must learn to thank God for everything you have been granted and then perhaps you will find peace. I can't stand your continual preaching, said his wife, packed her bags and left him for ever.

'4. An old religious man sensed that his last hour had come. If God would only grant me a sign before I die, he thinks to himself, I would die happy. Were you not happy before, then? God asks him. Happier, the man corrects himself. If God would only grant me a sign before I die I would die even happier than I have lived. What sort of sign did you have in mind? God asks him. Don't quibble, please, the man says, don't you see that I'm fading fast? I will have to think about it, God says, but the man, his face ashen, has only time to whisper, I always knew it would end like this, before the last breath leaves his body.

'5. When Cordelia made up her mind to answer her father as she did she was strengthened by the conviction that even if she had given up her rightful inheritance she had at least not sold her soul. Subsequently she discovered that the strength with which a belief is held is no guarantee of its truth.

'6. Homer tells us that Patroclus was killed by Hector when he entered the battle clad in Achilles' armour. What this reveals is that Patroclus was killed not because he was reckless but because, not satisfied with being himself, he wished instead to be Achilles.

'7. Two brothers were left a sizeable fortune by their father, which allowed them to do whatever they wanted for the rest of their lives. One of them decided to go into business, the other to become a painter. Both were moderately successful. One day the painter was found hanged in his studio. In his hand he clutched a piece of paper on which was written: "God knows, I tried." Forensic examination showed, however, that he could not have hanged himself. Further tests led to the conclusion that the note had been written by his brother. Though the latter protested his innocence to the last he was charged with murder and the death penalty imposed and carried out.'

The second manuscript consisted of a longer narrative, divided into three parts:

I

The English satirist and poet Jonathan Swift had, from his earliest days, been torn by two contradictory impulses: to have the world acknowledge his genius, and to have the world leave him alone. Always quick to see condescension where others saw merely friendship, he felt at ease in the company neither of men nor of women. Conscious of possessing powers quite out of the ordinary, he felt at the same time the extreme frustration of someone who has not been able to find an outlet for these powers. After an undistinguished career at the University of Dublin he took Holy Orders and came to England to make his name and fortune. Through family connections he attracted the attention of the ageing diplomat, Sir William Temple, who was at the time looking for an amanuensis to help him compile his memoirs and prepare his letters for posterity. Temple invited the young clergyman to live in his country house, Moor Park in Surrey, where he resided with his widowed sister and several dependants, including a young girl rumoured to be his natural daughter, Stella Johnson, and her companion, a certain Mrs Dingley. To the outside world Swift had at last fallen on his feet, but the young clergyman could not decide whether Sir William's attitude towards him was that of a kindly uncle or a harsh employer. And was he himself a trusty adviser or a mere household servant? Sir William worked him hard and if at times he took him into his confidence and treated him as one of the family, at others he seemed bent on making him recognise his place. Nor was it easy to see if his sister, Lady Giffard, was a friend or an enemy, an admirer intervening on his behalf with her self-obsessed brother, or a snob, determined that the young cleric should not gain any foothold in the affections of her illustrious brother.

Upon Sir William's sudden death Lady Giffard showed herself in her true colours by immediately dismissing the young amanuensis and refusing ever to see him again. After much effort Swift succeeded in obtaining a parish in Ireland, where he had himself been born. Somewhat to his surprise the two ladies, Stella and Dingley, followed him there.

II

Swift's literary career blossomed and, as he began to attract the attention of the country's leading politicians, so his relationship to the two ladies, who had taken up residence in Dublin, intensified. In the many months his political manoeuvrings kept him in London he wrote to them regularly in terms which indicate how close they had become. Against his will, it seemed, he now found himself grown dependent on another person, even though that dependence was always hedged about with irony and playfulness. It is even said that when he eventually returned to Ireland and settled in Dublin as Dean of St Patrick's Cathedral, he and Stella were married, but there is no certain proof of that. They continued to keep separate establishments and they continued to see a great deal of each other, but whether Swift kept his distance out of fear of the young woman or some deep need to be independent or a combination of both, it is impossible to say.

Stella's health had never been good, and soon it became evident that she was a sick woman. Swift, who feared illness almost as much as he feared giving up his independence, seemed to go out of his way to get sent to England when her illness grew worse. Tormented by fears of her impending death and by his sense of guilt at his treatment of her, he waited for news while keeping himself busy in London. At last the message he had so dreaded arrived: Stella was dying. He set out hurriedly for Dublin but missed the boat at Holyhead as his coach had been delayed on the way, and bad weather then made it impossible for him to cross for another week. Beside himself with anxiety, he spent the time roaming the coastal paths, getting drenched and lost, and sitting in his room at the inn writing down his thoughts about Stella, death and fate. He had wanted her and he had wanted his independence. Each alone would have allowed him to live in peace. Wanting both, he now felt, he had lost both. Yet he could have acted in no other way. God, he prayed, who made us what we are, give us the strength to endure whatever You have in store for us. When the weather at last cleared enough for him to get across to Dublin it was too late: Stella was dead.

III

Though he arrived in time for the funeral he did not attend it. Instead he sat in his rooms in the Deanery, next to the cemetery, writing down what he wished to be remembered of her and of his strange relationship with her. What he had sought all his life to avoid, the suffering entailed in parting from a loved one, had come to him in the end, and he had not even the satisfaction of recalling a life lived together to mitigate his suffering. And though he was still to write his greatest works, this realisation left him in

a sense a posthumous man. Since, however, that is what we are
all destined to become, he bore it with what equanimity he could,
though he confessed to the one friend who, he felt, would understand him, his fellow poet, Alexander Pope, that he had never had
a full night's sleep in his life again.'

Enclosed with these manuscripts Goldberg had written a kind
of dedication: 'To His Royal Majesty, this poor gift is offered in lieu
of his body by your most humble servant, Samuel Goldberg.'

17. Order

Tobias Westfield was not afraid of death, he was only afraid of unfinished business. He wanted to set his house in order but he did not know how to begin. Even worse, he did not even know what might constitute order, what might constitute a beginning.

– At your age! his friend Ballantyne said, to be always thinking of death!

Westfield turned his face away from him.

– You are an inveterate Romantic, Ballantyne said. You allow yourself to indulge in fantasies with names like Death, Order, Beginning and End. These have nothing to do with reality as we live it and you know that.

– I know it, Westfield said, and I know too that there must be more to life than your reality.

– When death comes, Ballantyne said, we will be too weak and befuddled to do more than simply submit to it. Meanwhile your life is ebbing away in your fantasies of order and meaning.

Westfield sensed that his friend was both right and wrong.

– We were not made simply to live for the moment, he said, else why should we have memories, why should we have the ability and the desire to formulate projects, why should we be filled with the need for order and for meaning in our lives?

– You know very well why, Ballantyne said, sitting back in his chair and looking at his friend under lowered lids. It is because we are afraid, it is because we have too much leisure on our hands, it is because we are weak and easily influenced by the foolish ideas that abound in society.

– I agree with you, said Westfield, that the peasant burdened by the need to work himself into exhaustion to feed himself and his family may not have the time for such thoughts, but does that mean that his life is the life we were all meant to live? Should we not hope rather that one day he too will be able to have the leisure the more fortunate amongst us now enjoy?

– That is what I am criticising, Ballantyne said. If you enjoyed your leisure all would be well, but it weighs on you like lead and fills your spirits with gloom.

– Do you mean to tell me, Westfield said, that you never lie awake at night tormented by the thoughts of what you might have done but did not do and what you have done which you ought never to have done?

– Did I say I alone did not partake of the universal weakness and susceptibility? his friend asked smiling. There are quite enough skeletons in my cupboard to keep me awake for a lifetime, if I allowed them to do so.

– You mean that by an effort of the will you do not allow them so to do? Westfield asked.

– I mean that I recognise such indulgences to be ultimately destructive, Ballantyne said, and I have no wish to destroy myself.

– Meaning what? Westfield asked him.

Ballantyne smiled and was silent.

There was something unsatisfactory about these exchanges, Westfield felt. They had known each other for so long, and each knew too well what the other would say before he had even opened his mouth. Is there a moment in most human relationships when this happens? he wondered. When both participants feel that something vital to the relationship has died? It is usual to describe the waning of love in these terms, but is it not even truer of friendship? Their relationship had hardened over the years until each felt that everything the other did or said he had already said or done many times before. The sense of the unexpected, which is the manure that nourishes human relations, had been exhausted and had not been replaced by anything new, though how and when that had happened neither would have been able to say. Westfield felt that he was confronting a machine, that something had died in his friend in the course of the years and now he only responded in a manner that was wholly predictable, in a parody of his old self. And he was too self-aware not to recognise that his friend must feel much the same about him.

Once, the discovery that their friendship was at an end would have saddened him immeasurably, for he had always felt that, whatever the vagaries of love, friendship at least was a solid rock in each man's affective life, and that his friendship with Ballantyne in particular, though it had been slow to form, had over the years grown remarkably strong. It had never occurred to him that it might one day wither and die, just as it had never occurred to him that he might one day find a conversation with him tedious and mechanical, so enchanted had he been by Ballantyne's character in the early days of their acquaintance. The thought then that their friendship could wane would have been unbearable, but now that it had, of course, he was merely indifferent.

– I had always imagined, Westfield said, that one could either die tragically, cut short with much still to be done, or that one could die old and full of years, as the Bible has it, after having put one's house in order. I had never considered that there is a third alternative, in which one went on living and yet found no order in one's life, in which everything at the end was as confused and unfinished as it had always been.

– The trouble with you, Ballantyne said, is that you have always had a hunger for stories. The life cut tragically short is a story, and the life satisfactorily completed is a story, as is the life of the insomniac who is lulled to sleep by sweet music. You have never been willing to face the fact that life is not a story, that the poets and novelists and playwrights have been lying to us since the dawn of creation and pandering to our fears and desires.

– I have no faith in God or in the theologies of the various religions, Westfield said, but I do have faith in life. I think we were meant to be active in the course of the day and to sleep soundly at night. But now I am beginning to doubt even that.

– That, said Ballantyne with a smile, if you will allow me to say so, comes from your never having been able to sleep soundly. We always idealise what we lack. I, on the other hand, who have never had a white night in my life, know full well that it is merely the result of a sound constitution allied to a clear view of what is in my best interest.

Westfield felt he could no longer stand the other's smugness. What had once seemed to him an admirable robustness now appeared to him like coarseness. He felt suddenly, as he had often felt in recent conversations with his friend, that he had sitting before him not a being of flesh and blood, exquisitely dressed for a visit, but a mere shadow, a ghost inside which a machine had been mechanically set in motion. And then he felt that he himself was not sitting in his well-lit study, gazing at his friend, comfortably ensconced in his favourite armchair, but was himself insubstantial, a being without shape or form, occupying no space.

– There have been moments, he said, making an effort to dispel the vision, when I seemed to accept who and what I was and felt myself to be living as I was meant to live. But these moments have grown rarer as the years have passed and now they are like a memory of another life.

Even as he spoke, though, he sensed that he was using the words *life* and *living* rather too often, and that Ballantyne, sitting in the chair opposite, seemed no longer even to notice that he was speaking. Why does he come? he wondered. Why does he sit there like that? Why does he go on with this charade?

Was this then the onset of old age? he wondered. Not even knowing if you exist any more? Not even knowing what you want any more? As if *want* was a word which he thought he knew but which now seemed to him simply a sound, robbed of all meaning. Like the word *order*. Like the phrase *to set your house in order*. But was his house not in order? His servants saw to that. He had made his will. He had done what he could for those for whom he had incurred responsibilities, his father, his wives, his dependants. As for his friends, he no longer had any. One after another they had all dropped away, as though friendship had become a burden which he had at first made every effort to shoulder and then had gradually realised that there was no need for and let go, and it had gone. Now even Ballantyne seemed dead to him. They were dead to each other and it was no use pretending otherwise.

And yet the loss affected him. He felt that if he had enough time he would be able to understand precisely why, but though he had nothing to do he seemed to have no time either any more. It was as if the feelings which had once lodged inside him, had been a part of him, were now dispersed about his pockets and there were too many pockets and they were too full for him to be able to sort out their contents, he would only feel himself being dragged down by their weight, distracted by the discomfort these dozens of pockets all stuffed full were causing him.

– If I had time, he said to Ballantyne, I would empty them out on the table in front of me and slowly and carefully go through them, putting together what belonged together, until I had everything in neat piles in front of me.

– I have absolutely no idea what you are talking about, Ballantyne said, smiling at him. Empty out what?

– My pockets. My pockets.

He had asked the musician to come and it had been no use. He had asked the writer to come and that had not worked. We are alone, he thought and it is only weakness to imagine that others will help us in our solitude. But that thought was no comfort to him, since he knew that he needed another to help him, that left to himself he would only knot himself up tighter and tighter until he was unable to think or feel or even breathe.

It will be better in the morning, he thought. It is always worse at this time of night. But if it was better in the morning it would be just as bad the following night, so that the slightest easing of his anxieties that came with the arrival of the dawn was no easing at all, a respite only, which, he now saw, merely made the inevitable relapse more painful, a joke played on him by his body. Now, as he lay in the dark, staring up from his bed, he felt himself outside time, the steady rhythm of every day which protected him from himself, felt that when he began to feel better in the morning he would already be aware of the moment when that feeling had worn off, and when every other feeling had also worn off, so that now he could face the truth and see that there was no hope at all, no hope from outside and no hope from within himself, that hope was folly and any thought of suicide was folly and he would simply have to go through with it, with whatever life had left to offer him. Am I the only one to have seen this? he wondered. Am I the only one to have felt this? No one, to his knowledge, even if they had seen and felt as he had, had ever committed that knowledge to writing. And how could they have? This knowledge was cold, ice-cold, and words were warm, words were imbued with human warmth which, he had just understood, was a sham and a deceit, words and writing were the very methods by which human beings had contrived to keep such knowledge from themselves. The ice bit into the words, made them grow stiff and then shatter in a thousand pieces.

Westfield turned over in his bed and sought a more comfortable position.

18. In the Carriage (3)

Jogging along in the carriage, – How much further we have to go? Goldberg asks his friend Hammond.

– Patience, Hammond says. Patience. We will get there in the end.

Goldberg makes to take his watch out of his waistcoat pocket but Hammond puts a restraining hand on his arm.

– No, he says. We will get there when we get there.

– True enough, Goldberg says.

He leans back in his corner of the carriage and closes his eyes. He thinks again about a fragment of dialogue he has recently written, an exchange between a man in his forties, a family man and a judge, and his young protegé, a fiery and confused young man of twenty-five.

– You profess a passion for music, the judge says to his young friend, so I would like you to consider the fugue.

The young man tries half-heartedly to conceal a yawn.

– What, asks the judge, is the basic characteristic of the fugue? Neither expecting nor waiting for an answer, he proceeds:

– The fugue is a piece of music in which there is no such thing as waste.

He pauses, aware that he has made an effect.

– Waste? his young friend says.

– Waste, the other repeats. A melody may be beautiful, he goes on, but it could always be otherwise than it is. A little extra trill here, a greater degree of accentuation there, still the same melody, roughly, but only roughly. The melody is haunted by the sense that it could be otherwise, that it is only one possibility among many, and therefore that it is in a sense profligate, throwing itself into the void, into the silence, when perhaps even the silence might have been better, might have been more effective. The shadow of the arbitrary and the wilful blights even its finest flowering.

The young man is silent. Gratified, the judge proceeds:

– But what is a fugue? he says. Etymologically it is a flight, of course. And if there is flight then there is a flee-er and a pursuer. When the one is identical to the other we have the basis of the musical art of fugue, which is the canon.

– But why do you see no waste in this then? the young man asks, growing suddenly interested.

– By doubling the melody all notion of waste is refined away, the judge says, as the old alchemists understood. Now the form of the one who flees is guaranteed by the form of the one who pursues. And the form of the one who pursues?

– By the form of the one who flees, the young man says.

– Exactly, says the judge. And as this happens a wonderful transformation takes place: since each is guaranteed by the other and each is no stronger or weaker than the other, no faster or slower than the other, there is no way in which the pursuer will catch up the one who is pursued, or the one who is pursued allow the pursuer to catch up. So the flight of the one from the other, which is really the flight of the solitary melody from itself, turns into the mutual respect of the one for the other, and into the physical pleasure of each in his own being, which is that of the other. The pursuer turns into the pursued and the pursued into the pursuer, and the headlong flight ceases to be a flight and becomes a dance.

The judge pauses to re-light his pipe.

– The essence of the fugue, he resumes when he has taken a few puffs and put away his matches, the essence of the fugue is dance, which means well-being in reciprocity. The essence of melody, even melody enlivened by harmony, is solitude and the melancholy of solitude.

– It could be the exhilaration of solitude, the young man says.

– Exhilaration inevitably followed by melancholy, the other

returns. Now, he says, I have been not been telling you about fugue in order to give you a lesson in music. You are far more interested in music than I am, and know far more about it than I do. No, he goes on, I have been telling you about music in order to illustrate the point I wished to make about marriage.

– Ah, the young man says with a sigh, I should have known.

– The point I wished to make about marriage, the judge goes on, is that the decision to make of your life only one part of a whole which is made up of two parts turns melancholy into joy and every second into a dance.

– But then the two parts have to be of one mind, the young man says with a smile.

– The decision to marry, the judge says, transforms what had been distinct into the parts of a whole. But, lacking such a decision, you remain prone to bouts of high exaltation followed by periods of gloom and depression. And the reason for this is the growing sense of waste, the feeling that everything you do could be done differently. And that, he says, leads easily to despair and to cynicism and indifference. All moods, or traits of character, I am not sure how to describe them, which you yourself have frequently confessed to being prone to.

– Let us understand each other, the young man says. I have nothing against marriage. On the contrary, I have a high, a very high regard for it. Nor do I willingly act the way I do or live the life I do.

– Then renounce it, the judge says. Give up the ways of indulgence and make your final choice.

– Nor, says the young man, not to be deflected, am I anything but an admirer, a passionate admirer, of canon and fugue. If I remember correctly, he adds, it was I who played for you generous selections from Bach's *The Art of Fugue*.

– And I acknowledge that, unmusical as I am, the judge retorted, I almost fell asleep as you were playing. However, he goes on, I was interested enough in the principles of the art of fugue to see that they constituted a powerful argument in favour of my view of marriage, and that your love of the form must be an indication that my attempts to persuade you of the correctness of those views would not fall on totally barren ground.

– You have, says the young man, given an eloquent account of the metaphorical potential of the fugue. Will you now consider further?

– In what way? asks the judge.

– Let me return first to what I was saying a moment ago, the young man says. There is no one who has a greater admiration than I do either for the institution of marriage or for the art of fugue. I am troubled, however, by your somewhat mystical comment that it is the decision which transforms everything. For how could a single decision do that? I have made many decisions in my life, and some I have adhered to, and some, alas, I have not, but in neither case has it transformed my life.

– Allow me, says the judge, raising his pipe.

– Of course, the young man says.

– There is only one decision in a man's life, the judge says. And that is the decision to let go of yourself and marry. Take that decision and your life is given back to you a hundredfold.

– Have I not heard that remark somewhere before? the young man says. Lose your life in order that you may gain it? And I was not aware, he says, that Our Saviour had been a married man.

– You choose always to misunderstand me, the judge says. In the Catholic Church of course to be a nun is to be married to Christ. The analogy of the fugue holds even here. And in the Protestant branches the sacred vocation of the priesthood and marriage are not deemed incompatible.

– So there is no other way? the young man asks. There is only the way of marriage to Christ or marriage to a woman?

– That is what I would say, the judge says.

The young man goes to the window, lifts the curtain and looks down into the street. After a while he lets fall the curtain and returns to his seat opposite his older friend.

– The canon, he says, can be considered as a form of permutation. But it is not the only such form. It is not even the main such form. Take the case of the farmer and his fields. Some he must allow to lie fallow, some he must sow, since they have lain fallow the previous year and are now ready. And it is well known that a field on which the same crop is sown, year in year out, even allowing for certain fallow years, will produce less and a poorer

quality of yield than the one in which crops are sown in strict rotation. This rotation method is of course a form of permutation, for
no crop should be sown before its turn has come, and no field lie
fallow before its turn. Thus if there are, say, five crops and one
field, and the ground should lie fallow for one year in six, it will be
simple to set up a rotation in which for six years the ground is
either fallow or has one of the five crops growing on it; with six
fields and twelve crops and the need to rest the fields once every
three years the problem grows a little more complex; with eight
fields, twenty-one crops and the need to rest the land once every
five years, it would tax the keenest mathematical mind to resolve
the problem.

   – Now, the young man says, given that in the course of a lifetime the average person is likely to meet more than one woman
to whom he wishes to bind himself for life, though not perhaps as
many as the thousands met with by Don Juan, would it not be
better for him to adhere to the rotation method rather than make
a single choice?

   – No, he says, holding up his hand as the other prepares to
speak. Let me finish. I am well aware of the fact that even six will
involve a choice. The farmer does not sow all the crops available
but only those which will bring him some tangible benefit, and
even here he may have to limit himself more or less arbitrarily.
But the point I am making, he says, is that the rotation method
emphasises the principle of arbitrariness rather more than does
the method of the fugue.

   – We disagree on this single principle of arbitrariness, the judge
interrupts him. For me the arbitrary choice of fugal partner only
remains arbitrary so long as it has not been made. Once it is made
the arbitrariness vanishes and necessity takes its place. It is like
the bestowal of a name on a baby, the judge continues. I pluck a
name out of the hat, or give the baby the name of my father. I call
him, let us say, Peter. Had my father been called Michael, he
would have been called Michael. But once he is named Peter or
Michael it is as if he had been so named from the creation of the
world.

   – I am not convinced by your analogy, the young man replies.
Though I grant that habit does somewhat blunt the edge of the

arbitrary. But to come back to your substantial point, can I commit myself in the way you suggest when I have only your word for it that it will transform my life?

– Do you not trust me? the judge enquires. Do you not see the ease and peace of mind in which I live? Do you not contrast daily your miserable and uncertain existence with mine and note my infinitely greater contentment?

– But how do I know that this is not the result of your temperament? his young friend asks. Or perhaps that you have been singularly fortunate in your choice of partner. What has worked for you might after all not work for me.

– It is a pity you did not know me in the days before my great decision to marry, the judge says. You would have seen that I was in every way like you.

– In that case, the young man says, I need take no decision, for if you were in every way like me and are now as I see you, I merely have to wait and I too will be like that. There is no need for you to try to persuade me and no need for me to pay attention to your views.

– No, the judge says. There was a great moment of decision. It was hard but I chose one thing when I might well – and I shudder to contemplate it – have chosen differently.

– But the fact that you chose as you did, the young man says, was, as I have already suggested, perhaps the result of your temperament, and also, perhaps, of the lady. My temperament may be different from yours and I may never meet a lady like your charming wife.

– That is the talk of the Devil, the judge says. That is the talk of those extreme sectarians who leave nothing to the free will of man.

– Perhaps it is the truth, the young man says, smiling.

– I warn you, the judge says. If you want to sleep at ease in your bed for the remainder of your life, listen to me. I beg you. Listen to me.

– But what if I do not want to sleep at ease in my bed? the young man asks.

– You spoke differently a while ago, the judge replies.

– True, the young man says. But how do we know what we really want? Let me put it like this, he goes on. There is no one who wishes more ardently than I to marry, and, as they say, to settle down. But there is also no one who is more aware of the impossibility of doing so as long as it does not seem to me imposed by necessity. Without that, it cannot be done.

– But the act imposes the necessity retroactively, the judge says.

– So we go round and round, the young man says, smiling.

– Only because you refuse to understand, the judge says.

– Or because you do, the young man says. There is one thing that worries me in your analysis of the fugue, he goes on. You describe it as a dance, as the realisation of freedom in necessity. That is very beautiful. But could it not also be seen as the annihilation of time and so of freedom? In the fugue I am always pursuing and the other always pursued, or I am always pursued and the other always pursuing, and each move I make and each move the other makes will always be repeated, for all eternity, for each of us is only the echo and mirror image of the other. That is my idea of Hell, not of Heaven.

– That too, the judge says, is the way I used to reason before I took the great decision. By taking the decision Hell was transformed into Heaven, mindless repetition into the freedom of reciprocity.

– We seem ourselves to have been playing the parts of a fugue, the young man says. I flee and you pursue me. Or perhaps you flee and I pursue you. Does that fill either of us with the joy of which you speak?

– Perhaps it fills God, who contemplates our conversation, with that joy, the judge retorts.

– Let us leave God and the Devil out of it, the young man says.

– If you prefer, the judge says, let us think of ourselves as being on a stage and looked at by an audience. I am happy to think that they will take pleasure from our dance. But only, of course, if at the end you follow my advice.

– But I can only squirm at the thought of having been overheard, the young man says. And at the thought that I have failed to make my position clear to you.

– On the contrary, the judge says. I understand you perfectly.

– Perhaps you only think you do, the young man says.

– Don't hide behind such thoughts, the judge says. I know the sense of waste you feel when you contemplate your life and I know the sense of happy necessity that guides mine.

– Can you not understand the perverse pleasure I take in contemplating that waste? the young man asks. And can you not understand how impossible it is to make a choice that seems only arbitrary?

The judge now gets up in his turn and goes to the window. He speaks with his back to the room.

– You are not the first young man to imagine that his feelings are unique, he says. You are not the first young man to wish to cling to his uniqueness at all costs, even at the cost of profound unhappiness.

– And if I am not, the young man says, should I then give up what I hold most dear?

– But what do you hold dear? the judge says. The melody imagines itself unique, it lovingly looks at itself in the mirror. The art of fugue banishes the mirror and brings life back into what was threatening to become a tomb.

– And what if the only life I can conceive is life in the tomb?

– That too, the judge says, is how one feels so long as the decision has not been taken.

– Do you wish to have the last word at all costs? the young man asks smilingly.

– That is my privilege as your senior, the judge says, smiling in his turn. Though the joy of the art of fugue is that words like first and last lose all their meaning.

Goldberg opens his eyes and looks out of the window. The English countryside rolls past, unchanging.

– How much longer? he asks.

– Patience, my dear Goldberg, patience, Hammond says. We are making good progress.

– How much longer? Goldberg persists.

– Who can tell? Hammond says. We will arrive when we will arrive.

▐

19. Back in London

Back in London I tried to get on with my work as though nothing had happened. After all, the end was almost in sight. But it was as if Como and Basle belonged to another world. Those dreadful few minutes in the Unterlinden Museum had changed everything.

There had been no word from Edith. I had no idea where she was, how she was living, what she was doing. Every day I expected her to turn up and tell me it had all been a mistake, a momentary aberration, but day followed day and I heard nothing from her. When Larry rang to ask how the holiday had been I told him what had happened.

– She just walked out? he said.

– Yes, I said.

– With no explanation?

– No.

– How do you feel about it? he asked.

– How do you expect me to feel?

– You hadn't quarrelled?

– No.

– There isn't another man?

– I thought of that, I said. Of course. But she denies it.

– Poor Dad, he said.

– I don't, I said, blame your mother in the least. Nor do I blame myself. These things happen.

– Fuck it Dad, he said. Blame her. Blame her. Or yourself. This neutrality pisses me off.

Where did my children acquire such a vocabulary? Such a way

of expressing themselves?

– Larry, I said, you're thirty years old. Do you have to speak like that?

– Fuck it Dad, he said. Get angry. Get mad. But don't give me that politeness shit, right?

I put the phone down and went back to my desk. But it rang again at once and it was still Larry.

– Dad, he said. Talk like a human being, will you? And don't hang up on me like that.

I put the phone down again, then took it off the hook. What have I done to deserve such children? Full of American street jargon and cod psychology.

Later Miriam called me.

– Larry told me, she said. He said you were so angry you wouldn't even talk to him.

– I'm not angry, I said. I'm puzzled. I'm upset. Wouldn't you be?

– Perhaps she needed to do that, she said.

– Why needed?

– You don't know why?

– No, I said.

– Then that's why, she said.

These children. These psychologists. Such banality.

– Do you want me to come round? she said.

– Come round? I said. Why?

– I thought you might like to see me.

– Of course I'd like to see you. But not so you can explain her actions to me. They are inexplicable and inexcusable.

– No they're not, she said.

– All right, I said. They're not.

– We've often wondered how she could put up with you, Dad, she said. And don't think I'm passing judgement.

– Not passing judgement? I said. What the hell are you doing then?

– I'm just stating the facts, she said.

– Your mother walks out on me after thirty-three years of married life, I say, and it's me you blame?

– No one's blaming you, she said. Can't you understand that?

– You'll excuse me for thinking that's just what you're doing, I said.

– Oh come off it, Dad, she said.

– That's the position then, I said. Your mother has vanished. She's probably sunning herself in Bali with Georg Haverkampf.

– What?

– Someone we met, I said.

– And she went off with him?

– It's possible, I said. Everything seems to be possible these days. I can't quite see what's in it for him, but stranger things seem to happen round us all the time

– You know this for a fact? she said.

For a fact! Why can't she speak English? Who taught her to speak like that?

– No, I said. She may be anywhere with anyone or nowhere with no one.

– What does that mean? she said.

– If you're so anxious about her, I said, get in touch with Interpol.

– Oh come off it, Dad, she said.

– If you'll excuse me, I said, I've got to get on with my work.

– Give us a call as soon as you hear anything, will you, Dad? she said.

Why does my daughter always say 'we' and 'us'? She always has. As though she was afraid of saying anything in her own right. Now she's married I don't know if she means 'my brother and I' or 'my husband and I' or whether she means anything at all. I suspect she doesn't know herself.

I tried to work. After all, in Como, in Basle, I had felt I was in the home straight. The thing I resented most was Edith doing what she had done without any thought for the state of my work. I had always thought she respected it and respected what I was trying to do, but this showed she was as selfish as the rest of them. Three more weeks and I would have done it. Three more weeks of quiet sustained work in London without any distractions and I would have brought three years' work to a conclusion. Not perhaps a totally successful conclusion, that would have been too much to hope for, but a conclusion nonetheless. What right did she have to throw this bombshell just at the most delicate stage?

I pride myself on being able to work in any circumstances. Years ago Saul Bellow criticised me for saying I could no longer write longhand, so needed to lug my typewriter around with me everywhere. A writer should be able to write anywhere, in any circumstances, he growled as he smiled his charming smile. After all, he went on, all a writer needs is a stub of pencil and a piece of paper. I was so struck by this that I forced myself to revert to longhand and to scribble away in planes and trains and crowded tubes. Nowadays of course everyone carries a laptop, but I suspect Saul still has his pencil. What Edith had done, though, was to ensure that the book would not get finished. Perhaps that was her intention. Perhaps all those years when I thought she was supportive she had secretly envied or – who knows? – even despised my work. And now she had planned this so as to cause maximum damage. No. I don't think she had planned that. I can't believe it of her. Indifference, yes. Lack of thought, yes. But not deliberate sabotage. I would never believe that of her. I couldn't believe that of her. And I still expected her back.

That was really what made writing so impossible. Every day I sat down at my desk and forced myself to work, but I had lost the thread. If I had been sure Edith would never come back I might have been able to concentrate. But I was in limbo. Waiting. And nothing can be done in states like that. I tried reading Homer and listening to Bach, which usually brought me back in touch with the reality of what I was trying to do, but Homer seemed incomprehensible and Bach had never sounded more like what Colette once called him, 'cette divine machine à coudre'. How had they ever spoken to me? Why had I never thought I could write my book in their shadow? And the contemporary fiction I picked up, the contemporary music I listened to on the radio, meant nothing to me either.

The trouble was I could think only about my book, yet I had lost the spark that would keep me going. I tried to recall the excitement of seeing the *Wander-Artist* in the Haverkampf collection, but though I could see the image clearly in my mind's eye, it no longer said anything to me. I propped the postcard on my desk and gazed at it, I examined the marks of Klee's brushstrokes, the black of the frame, the red of the figure, but it was no good, familiarity had robbed it of speech. I went for walks round London with it in my pocket and took it out on buses and in cafés and glanced at it and quickly put it back, but I felt all the time that I was playing a game with myself, that I was no longer in touch with reality, with its reality, with my reality, with the novel's reality.

One day Leila Haverkampf phoned me. Her voice on the phone was quite different from the voice I remembered, but when she said who it was I immediately conjured up the image of her at one and the same time hoisting the little gold-rimmed glasses back up her nose and pushing the hair back from her face.

– Where are you? I asked.

– Oh, she said, here in Berne.

– Are you coming to London? I asked stupidly

– Would you like me to? she asked.

– Me? I said, but she was silent at the other end.

– Me? I said again, stupidly.

I waited for her to tell me what she was phoning about, but she was silent.

– How are you? I asked at last.

– Oh, she said, fine. Just fine.

– Good, I said.

– And Edith?

– Have you seen her? I asked.

– Seen her? she said. Why should I have seen her? Is she not with you?

– No, I said.

I waited for her to ask for an explanation, and when she didn't I asked how Georg was.

– He's fine, she said.

– He's with you?

– With me?

– I mean, is he travelling a lot?

– No, she said. Not more than usual.

– I see, I said

– I wanted to tell you abut something that happened to me recently, she said.

I waited, curious.

– I was walking in the meadows above the house, she said, and I saw a most beautiful butterfly. It was green and blue, colours I had never seen on a butterfly in that combination before. I watched it as it flew low over the grass and flowers of the meadow, she said, and then it rose up and flew towards me and before I knew what had happened it had flown into my ear.

– Into your ear? I said.

– Yes, she said.

– And then? I said.

– It flew straight into my ear, she said, and on into my head. It is still there.

– Still there in your head?

– Yes, she said.

I waited for her to go on. She was silent.

– What are you going to do about it? I said foolishly.

– Nothing, she said. There is nothing that can be done about it.

– Have you consulted a doctor? I asked.

– A doctor would not be any use.

– I see, I said.

– I wanted to tell you, she said. It is green and blue. In an unusual combination for a butterfly, in my experience. It is flying around inside my head.

– Yes, I said, I see.

– I just wanted to tell you, she said.

– Why?

– I wanted to, she said. And now I must ring off. I find it difficult to speak for any length of time on the telephone with a butterfly in my head.

– Yes, I said foolishly. Yes, I see.

– Goodbye, she said.

– Goodbye, I said.

She rang off.

Afterwards I sat at my desk and thought about our conversation, but it made no more sense in retrospect than it had done at the time. I thought of phoning her back and trying to find out just why she had decided to call me, and even went so far as to open my address book and check whether or not I had the number, but then I closed it again and sat staring at the postcard of the *Wander-Artist* propped up on my desk. Perhaps when I finished the book. Until then, I thought, no distractions. One last push, I thought and then see what the world has to offer. One last push. But who would give the pusher a push?

20. Sleep

I went in at last to Mr Westfield. I was very calm. The servant brought me to the door, knocked, and then opened it and stepped aside for me to enter.

As on the first night the door to his room was open but the room itself was in darkness. I stood in the doorway of the antechamber and waited. After a while I heard him say:

– Come in, Mr Goldberg, come in. Do not stand upon ceremony.

I entered a little further into the room.

– Sit down, Mr Goldberg, sit down, he said.

I sat down and waited.

– Well? he called out at last.

– Would you like me to begin, sir? I enquired.

– If you would, Mr Goldberg. I would be most grateful.

I drew the sheaf of papers from my pocket.

– No, he said. Wait.

I waited.

– Step inside my room, he said. You will find a chair on the right hand side of the room.

I got up and did as he bade me. Once I had crossed the threshold of the room I was in total darkness, but my outstretched hand very soon encountered the chair of which he had spoken. I felt my way round it and sat down.

– Now we are both in the dark, he said, and, being in the same room, do not need to shout to make ourselves heard.

I sat there, waiting.

– You have written something? he asked.

– I have.

– Do you need to read it or will you be able to recite it to me in the dark?

– I will need to read it.

– A pity, he said.

He was silent so long I thought he had fallen asleep or forgotten me, but finally he said:

– Music seems to come from no source, but words always imply a speaker, do they not, Mr Goldberg?

He was not really asking for confirmation, so I remained silent.

– It is a great pity music moves me as little as it does, he said. Perhaps it is because I never really mastered its rationale.

– In my youth, he said, I loved to listen to music and could even play a little myself.

– But you did not persevere? I asked.

– Alas, no, he said. Other things intervened. Besides, I reached a point when I realised that I would never be able to understand it. To understand it inwardly, if you grasp my meaning. That I was a word-person, not a note-person.

– Perhaps it is a mistake to be too absolute, I ventured.

– Absolute?

– To decide once and for all that one is this and not that, that one can do this and not that, and so on.

He thought about this.

– Perhaps, Mr Goldberg, he said at last. But I am, and nothing can be done about it.

I waited for him to question me, if that is what he wished to do.

– Are you not yourself similarly absolute? he asked.

– I try not to be, I said.

– And you succeed?

– Sometimes, I said.

– There you are, he said.

We sat in silence in the dark.

– They have looked after you well? he asked me.

– I have had all I want, I replied.

– I have thought much about your visit, he said. Does that surprise you?

– No sir, I said.

– I am much given to thought, he said. It is my only indulgence.

– I am sorry to hear it, I said.

He laughed at that.

– A man may think as much as he pleases, he said, and no one can gainsay him. It is different with other indulgences, as you must be aware.

I did not think he wished for a response and so gave none. Suddenly he said:

– Is there to be no end to thought?

– No end? I echoed, surprised by his vehemence.

He did not respond.

– The poet Hölderlin has written, I said, that 'Where there is danger salvation grows there too'.

– What are you trying to tell me? he said.

– Perhaps thinking as much as one pleases is precisely what is wrong with thinking, I said.

He was silent, but I felt he was listening intently.

– Perhaps the lack of danger in thought is precisely what is so terrible about it, I said. Is precisely what links it to despair.

– You think I am in despair, Mr Goldberg?

I said nothing, struck by the sound of the words in the thick darkness.

– Do you? he pressed me.

– A kind of despair, I said.

– A kind? he said quickly. Does despair then come in many forms?

– Like love, I said.

– Ah, he said. Then he was silent.

I waited, but he seemed disinclined to speak, or perhaps he was digesting what I had just said.

– Perhaps, I said, the reason you cannot sleep is because you cannot really wake up.

– I have been awake all my life, he said.

I was silent.

– But I think I understand what you are saying, he said.

He was silent again, and I waited, seated at my ease in the deep chair.

– And you have something in your pocket that will wake me? he said suddenly, laughing.

– No, I said.

– No?

– That would be too much to ask.

– But that is what I am paying you for, he said.

– You are paying me to read to you, I said.

– True, he said, a note of sadness in his voice.

After a while he said:

– Do you think I will ever wake up then?

– I cannot tell.

– But you can venture an opinion.

– That is what I have done, I said.

He was silent again. Then he said quietly:

– Perhaps I have really been asleep all my life.

I waited in the darkness.

– Is there no way you can help me? he asked at last.

I took my time.

– No, I said.

– You were my last hope, he said.

He was silent for a long time.

– I am horribly afraid, he said finally.

I did not respond.

– And you, Mr Goldberg?

– Me?

– You are never afraid?

– I have my work, I said.

– Putting words together?

– If you like.

– Yes, he said, and was silent again.

– You make no effort to comfort me, he finally said.

– No, I said.

– I am not afraid of death, he said. Or solitude. I am only afraid of drifting into death unawares.

– We all of us will do that, I said.

– All? he said. You think so?

– Perhaps we should not call it drifting, I said.

– Then what word would you use?

– I mean, I said, that we must let these things take their course.

– Let the current take the boat where it will?

– If you like, I said.

– I had not thought of it like that, he said.

– We should not be frightened of death, I said. We should not demonise it.

He was silent.

– You have seen a dead bird, I said, lying in the grass? Perhaps you have on occasion picked one up and buried it. There is nothing to be afraid of there. It is the same with human beings.

He was silent for a long time.

– Perhaps, he said finally, I have always had too much money to encounter danger, in the terms of your friend.

– Not my friend, I said, but a great poet.

He was silent again.

– I do not think it is a matter of money, I said.

– Then of what?

– Of an attitude to the present, I said.

– The present?

– I have the feeling, I said, and you will forgive me, sir, if I am speaking out of turn, that your life has always been governed by a kind of anxiety and that in order to overcome that anxiety you have constantly rushed forward, in both thought and deed, instead of allowing each moment its full value.

– Go on, he said quietly, since I had come to a stop.

– Each moment, for you, I said, has only been a bridge between one thing and another. You call that thinking. I would prefer to call it anxiety.

– But what if I was born anxious? he said. How can I change myself?

– It does not matter where the anxiety has come from, I said. We can always find things to blame: our fate, our parents, our wives, our children. The important thing is to locate the cause and see if we can eradicate it.

He was silent. I did not know whether to go on or not. I said:

– Do you hear my voice?

– Yes, he said. Of course.

– Do you hear your own?

He was a long while answering. Then he said, very quietly:

– Yes, I think so.

– In the dark, I said.

I could sense that now he was waiting for me to continue.

– That is enough, I said.

– Yes, he said.

After a long time he said:

– This is the moment, then?

– It is, I said.

– Now?

– Yes.

– Our two voices in the dark?

I was silent.

– Nothing more?

– No.

I did not move. His breathing grew deeper.

– I see, he said again, after a while, in a whisper.

The silence around us was absolute, broken only by his steady breathing. I turned my head a little and saw the open doorway, dimly lit by the light burning in the antechamber.

– I see, he said once more, his voice now barely audible.

His steady breathing filled the room. I waited, afraid that if I moved I would wake him. But eventually I stood up, making as little noise as I could. He did not stir.

I felt my way towards the door, stopping at every step to hear if his breathing had altered, but I need not have worried.

I stood in the doorway for an instant, aware that if he was awake he would see my silhouette outlined against the light from the antechamber and would call out. His breathing came to me steadily through the darkness.

I turned and tiptoed to the door of the antechamber. Still he did not call me back. I opened the door and stood for a while with my hand on the knob, then quickly stepped out into the corridor and pulled the door shut after me.

21. The Lord of Time

Mr Tobias Westfield sat at his window and looked out at the park. His thoughts turned to Goldberg. How does a Jew live? he wondered. How does a writer live? I should have asked about the rituals he performs, he thought. I should have asked him about his methods of work. What thoughts came to him as he lay in bed at night? he wondered. A musician he could understand, though he was not musical himself, but a writer? Did he sit down at his desk every day and compose the perfect page? Or did he scribble for hours and then tear it all up? I should have asked him how he knew when a work was finished, he thought. I should have asked him how he knew what was the start. When he has gone, he thought, I will talk to Ballantyne about him, and then he remembered that he and Ballantyne hardly talked any more. Does he walk hand in hand with his wife, he wondered, even now they are no longer young?

Westfield had corresponded with some of the greatest writers in Europe and had even met one or two of them, but their relationship had always been clearly prescribed: he was simply one of many admirers with whom the great writer corresponded or to whom he deigned to offer an interview. But Goldberg was different. He was a man like himself, flesh and blood, a man with daily worries and, no doubt, bodily ailments. Yet he too was a man apart. He was a paid hireling, yet he retained a distance, a dignity, the distance and dignity of a man in charge of his own destiny. How had he acquired this? What was it that had made him what he was? His faith? But faith in what? In his God or in his work?

Westfield gazed out of the window and saw nothing. He

remembered his own attempts at writing, his own schemes and fantasies. They had always seemed hurried, snatched from the jaws of time though he had nothing more pressing to attend to. Goldberg, on the other hand, struck him, even at a first meeting, as someone not subject to time in that way, someone in fact who was the lord of time and not its slave. The lord of time, he thought, what a strange phrase to pop into my head. And yet it seemed apposite, even accurate. The lord of time, he said again, and watched a squirrel glide across the lawn. Is one born with that? he wondered. Does it come about by dint of hard work or is it passed on to you by your parents?

He is a man who understands, he thought, and then: But understands what? Perhaps that's it, he thought, he understands. Not this or that, but simply understands. A man not burdened by heredity or property, a man wedded to his profession. He had not found in Goldberg either the servility of a hireling or the conceit of a man to whom fame has come early in his lifetime, he suddenly thought. He is a man I can talk to, he thought, yet talk to differently from the way I used to talk to Jack Ballantyne. With Ballantyne, he thought, it was always the conversation of two men stuck on a raft together and being swept out to the edge of the rapids. We propped each other up, he thought, but Goldberg needs no propping up. He is a man who sleeps well because that is how his body functions.

Watching the squirrel holding up a nut between his front paws, Westfield pondered the enigma of Goldberg. I do not know where he comes from, he thought, and I do not know where he is going, but the strange thing is that he seems merely present. As though coming and going were not concepts applicable to him.

Westfield got up and went over to his glass. He gazed at himself for a while, then went back and sat down at the window. The prologue is over, he thought. The prologue of my life is over. Now there is only the epilogue left.

The squirrel had gone. And even the image of Goldberg, which had only a second ago been so vivid in his mind had begun to fade. Am I lying on my bed in the dark, he wondered, and only imagining myself sitting at the window? Or am I really sitting at the window and for some reason have begun to imagine myself once again lying on my bed in the dark? Who is Goldberg? he thought. Who am I? And it came to him, fleetingly, that there was no answer to such questions, that the problem lay in imagining that there was, and for a brief moment he knew what it felt like for it not to matter.

22. In the Dark

It is a pleasure to have you here, Mr Goldberg.

No no. Please do not try to be polite. You are here because I am paying you.

That is true.

That is true as well.

Civilised conversation does a man good.

Particularly civilised conversation in the dark.

I have often thought that if only we knew what it was we needed we would all be happy.

True, but in many cases the wherewithal is there, only men fail to understand what it is they want or need.

Yes, sometimes it is very little.

Very little indeed.

Very true. I shall remember that: Only when we have acquired it do we know that it is what we want.

Yes, need.

Yes. The more wealth and leisure we have the more difficult it is to know what we really need.

That is true in my case. How different might my needs have been if my first wife had not died so soon and so suddenly.

Yes. Each fresh blow brings with it an altered need.

Do you think so? Do you think then that such needs are innate or called up by the events of earliest childhood?

Perhaps. Perhaps you are right.

Has that been the case with you, sir?

That is true. Even money cannot buy everything.

Kant said that?

I would not wish to intrude. I merely thought we were speaking as friends.

Kant said that too? About the buying of friends? What did Kant not say, Mr Goldberg, what did he not say?

That has been my weakness. A failure of the creative capacity has led to an undue reliance on the wisdom of others.

You think so? Perhaps I do not know myself as well as I thought. But you, Mr Goldberg, speak like one who does.

Only because you recognise that you are not? Was that not Socrates' answer?

Very true. Very true. After all, someone somewhere must have said that before.

You think so? You think it does not matter?

In my case, the recognition that music does not speak to me.

Yes, yes. I can enjoy a rousing tune, but it does not speak to me as I know it does to others. After a few notes I find that my mind is not engaged. I find that far from soothing it irritates me. It has taken me half a lifetime to discover this.

Two thirds perhaps.

I have tried drink but it only sickens me. I have not the liver for excessive drinking.

And travel too. In my youth I travelled extensively. But it had, if anything, the contrary effect. Only here, in my own house, in my own bed, is there even a remote chance that I will be able to fall asleep.

No. Physical exercise too only seems to stimulate my mind, not calm it.

I am an optimist, Mr Goldberg. In spite of everything I am an optimist. I feel that one day I will find the right solution.

We are alone, Mr Goldberg. However much we flap and try to deny it, we must eventually recognise that truth And yet we were not made to be alone. We have outlived our time, Mr Goldberg. I sometimes feel that I am the first of a new breed of men. That when all men are like me the race of men will pass from the earth.

If you knew my circumstances, Mr Goldberg, you would not speak thus.

Indeed. One of my sons is a fool and the other an idiot. I fail to see myself in either.

I mean that one imagines that I have slighted him and denied him from his earliest years and his only wish is to get even with me, while the other, alas, is quite cut off from the world.

No. At first we hoped he would improve. We welcomed every word he said and imagined it would be the prelude to more, but gradually even those few words seemed to fade from his mind and soon he became completely silent.

If you saw him you would not say that, Mr Goldberg.

No. It is not a topic I wish to dwell upon. But tell me about your own.

Envy, fortunately, is not one of my vices.

No, I have never been envious of any man. I am perhaps too well aware of the folly of it.

Clarity of mind has always been one of the things I prided myself on.

It is possible to despair and yet remain an optimist.

Yes. Despair is a state, optimism a condition.

It is very simple. I see myself as though on an island of optimism in a sea of despair.

Lack of hope. Lack of hope.

You think so? I had never heard that before. Despair as a form of self-indulgence? I wish it were.

Because then I could free myself from it.

Not as simple as that? Mr Goldberg, our conversation in the dark is doing me more good than I could have imagined.

A kind of leaden echo.

That is true. That is why talking to you is doing me so much good.

I have often thought about it. I believe it was always there.

Even as a child.

Yes, even as a baby. Well, let us leave babies out of it. But as a child, certainly.

Her death only confirmed it. It seemed that I had always known it would be so. That I had perhaps been half expecting it, though hiding that expectation from myself, of course.

You think not? But I am telling you it was so.

You would know me better than I know myself?

As well?

Your confidence amazes me, Mr Goldberg.

Yes, you have said that before. We have mentioned Socrates.

Why should I relish it? It ruins my days and my nights as well.

Perhaps I have not made myself clear. It is not something I think about the whole time. It is like a fine web which surrounds me. Like the air I breathe.

I am aware of that, Mr Goldberg. But to know the doctrines of the faith does not necessarily mean that one can believe them.

That one can act? Without believing?

To forget about belief? I had not thought in those terms before.

Perhaps you are right. Perhaps there is something exciting in the knowledge that I have in some sense passed over to the other side, though I still draw breath.

I do not think so.

One goes on, Mr Goldberg, one goes on.

Perhaps one imagines it will some day stop while knowing full well that it will not.

Of course. Of course. My books. My correspondence. My house. All that is cause for immense satisfaction.

Yes. That too. That is why when the musician proved inadequate I thought of you.

Your fame has spread far and wide.

No, no. Do not contradict me. Far and wide.

Everybody I talked to. Believe me, I made extensive enquiries.

Perhaps.

I am naturally curious. That is what makes my despair bearable. I always wonder what else is in store.

Indeed. Hume. Voltaire. Goethe. In the morning I will show you.

Gibbon. Voltaire. No, with Herr Goethe I have only corresponded.

No. You are the first.

I never thought they were any different. Men like us. But with, perhaps, your own distinctive way of looking at things.

Your sufferings.

Of course. But your ancestors. Your co-religionists elsewhere in Europe. I have a knowledge of history, Mr Goldberg, I am a student of human nature.

Yes. I understand. One does not want to become lachrymose.

Yes, of course. One does not want to become embittered. I quite take your point. But you must think of these things yourself, sometimes, must you not?

Forward, yes, I suppose so.

Me? I have nothing to look forward *to*, Mr Goldberg. Nothing except old age and death.

That is well said. I will remember it. The short perspective not the long, tomorrow, not the rest of my life. Yes. I see exactly what you mean by the short perspective.

Yes, that is true.

No. My eyes are open and looking out into the darkness.

On three sides only. The side nearest the door is drawn back.

Shutters and curtains.

Yes. One is distracted by a type of coat one has not seen before. Or by the effort of looking into the eyes.

Precisely.

Writing is like that? Like speaking in the dark? I never thought of that.

And reading too?

But even granted that, my life is still my life.

Very true, Mr Goldberg, very true.

Bishop Berkeley, of course. But I had not…

Yes, I see. Though that seems somewhat presumptuous.

Each writer himself the voice of poetry? No longer X or Y… Yes I see.

Of course. And that is why Shakespeare has always seemed so pre-eminent and so enigmatic… Everyone and no one. Yes. Inhabiting the different forms and leaving them transformed. How well you put it.

A kind of celestial duet you say? *Our* conversation? Surely that –

If one could only see the contours, free of the content. You please me greatly, Mr Goldberg.

No, no. I did not say flatter. I said please. I am perfectly well aware of the fact that you do not flatter. That it is not, in a sense, me, Westfield, or you, Goldberg, you are talking about, but our two voices rising into the silence and then vanishing again into it.

Indeed, everything, even the plays of Shakespeare, will one day vanish.

Have already?

Yes, I see, you are still trying to wean me from my human perspective.

Both? I do not see… ?

No. Try as I may I cannot be both myself and not myself.

Perhaps, as you say, one day…

Another paradox?

But if one is speaking one is speaking and if one is silent one is silent!

Not to speak is to be noisy?

Ah, but that is a kind of speech we must surely leave to the angels…

Metaphorically speaking, metaphorically speaking.

Who is to say? Well, I am for one.

Not me? You would enmesh me deeper perhaps than I wish to go, Mr Goldberg.

I do not quite understand. To speak out into the dark, not knowing beforehand what one is going to say, allows the contours of the self to emerge?

Not to emerge but to… ?

I see. Emerge suggests they are there but invisible, so to speak, till they are… Whereas you mean that one makes such contours as one speaks…

And sleep?

A kind of speech as well?

The speech of the body in the mind of God? That is too mystical for me, Mr Goldberg.

Every gesture and every moment throughout the whole course of one's life? I begin to see what you are saying, Mr Goldberg. Every gain and every loss a comma and a full stop. So that there would be no more remorse and no more self-criticism, because it would be as it had to be, yet not fated but chosen, yet not chosen by the will but by something deeper, and each person would be what he is because he could not be other and have done as he did because he had to and the sorrows too and the disappointments a part of the whole, the sense that it could have been other and yet what it was...

　　It is strange, Mr Goldberg, for a moment as I spoke I was no longer myself but you.

　　And you me?

　　Yes. Perhaps you are right. So that there is no longer...

　　No longer...

　　So that there is no

23. Dear Edith

Dear Edith,

I can't go on. God knows I tried. But without you I find I simply can't go on.

Dear Edith,

I have hesitated for a long time before writing this but now I can hesitate no longer. Your selfish and thoughtless action that day in Colmar and your subsequent silence have effectively put paid to my book. I tried for weeks to ignore what had happened, feeling convinced at moments that it was only a temporary aberration on your part and you would soon return, and at others that these merely contingent events, these results of what Nietzsche called 'back-stairs psychology', should in no way interfere with the much more important business of finishing my book. But unfortunately these things are far more closely intertwined than I had imagined and the effect of your strange and inexplicable action has been to make me lose the momentum I had so painstakingly acquired in the course of our holiday. The book simply will not come alive for me again. I have tried everything, but it refuses to budge. I cannot go on and the future looks very bleak. I will probably leave this place but where I will go I have as yet no idea. I had thought

Dear Edith,

Though you appear to have severed all links with me I thought I should put you in the picture. The book has collapsed under me again. I tried for a while to keep it going but it became clear as I struggled with it that the flaw at its heart, which I had already sensed last year but which our holiday and the renewed energy it gave me had served to paper over, was central and profound. I cannot go on with it. I will try to forget it and turn to something else, but whether, after working on it for all those years, I can succeed in this is another matter.

Dear Edith,

I will leave this with Larry in case you should take it into your head to return. I do not know what you are up to, nor do I much care, frankly. I am selling the house and clearing out.

Dear Edith,

I will leave this with Larry for him to pass on to you should you ever give your children sign of life. Leila Haverkampf and I are going to settle in France. Once we have found a house I will let the children know and they can pass on the information to you. I'm sorry it had to end as it did but no doubt it was my fault as much as your own. I was too taken up with my own work to realise how you felt. It has, however, worked out for the best, for me at any rate. I hope you too will find peace and satisfaction, wherever you are and whatever your plans.

24. Goodbye, My Darling, Goodbye

My dear. I have been dreaming here this last hour. Time is running out and soon I must go and perform for my new patron. I have still got nothing prepared and seem unable to turn my mind to it. What shall it be? What kind of tale will send him to sleep? Without realising it he has set me a fiendish conundrum. If what I say bores him he will simply dismiss me in anger and frustration. On the other hand if it excites him too much he will want to listen through to the end, and when it is over he will be wide awake and eager for more.

I little thought when I accepted the commission that it would turn out like this. I imagined I would read to him from one of the many books I had brought with me and that as I read he would relax his grip on present reality, enter the world of my tale, then gradually drift off to sleep. But, as I have already explained to you, he would have none of that, he did not want me to read from any of the books I had brought with me. Instead he insisted that I write something specially for the occasion. He dropped in this new demand as though that were the simplest thing on earth. And for him no doubt it seems to be. And a part of me agrees with him. Why should I not write something? My invention is as good as the next man's, and my ability to formulate ideas and to construct narrative better than most. What is it then that has held me back throughout the day in a kind of dream? Why have I done everything, it seems, except the one thing needful?

The manservant has been in and brought me my dinner. He has told me I have but two hours before the master expects me.

The food was plain but good. It will perhaps be my last meal here, for I cannot see how I can retain my position if I do not perform as I am expected to. We will have to postpone the roofing. I wonder if any other commissions have arrived in my absence? Though if word gets round, as it is bound to, that I have failed here, what is to become of us?

I have been thinking about sleep and about how like breathing it is. Those of us who fall asleep without difficulty, like those of us who breathe without effort, think nothing of it. It is only when, for some reason, it is withheld, that it comes to seem so precious. But of course at any moment we could all become one of those for whom sleeping, or breathing, is a problem.

We spend a third of our lives asleep, if we are among the lucky ones, and yet, curiously, very little has been made of sleep in the literature of the past. For obvious reasons. It is not interesting. Nothing happens. Only dreams, or the inability to sleep, are interesting. But does that not tell us something about art? It purports to speak of man and all his doings, but in effect it speaks only of those things most amenable to speech. Homer, of course, is the exception in this as in everything else. Indeed, sleep could be said to be the secret theme, perhaps even the secret goal, of both his *Iliad* and his *Odyssey*. In the former Achilles will not sleep until he has been avenged first on his own comrades who, he feels, have inflicted shame upon him, and then on Hector, who has killed his dear friend Patroclus. But even then, even when Hector is dead and he has been reconciled to the other Argives and even to Agamemnon, something still keeps him awake. Only giving back the body of Hector to his grieving father finally allows the rage and anger to evaporate, to leave him and to leave the poem, so that both hero and poem can at last fall asleep in peace. And is not the climax of the *Odyssey* the return of Odysseus to his beloved wife and to his own secret bed? Then at last both he and the poem can fall asleep.

And what does this suggest? Why, simply this, that sleep is the goal of art as it is of man. And it can only be the sleep that truly ends if it has in some way been earned by the protagonist and earned by the writer. In that sense it is also the goal of the reader. But only a true work will allow him to sleep well when he has closed the book. He will not be fooled. His body will not be fooled.

He will know if the sleep of the end has been truly earned or not.

With Shakespeare we are already in the modern world. He conveys powerfully the torments of the guilty soul, robbed of sleep by reason of the deeds he has committed or the jealousies that torment him. He shows us the noble king, guardian of his people, taking upon himself their anxieties and fears so that they may sleep in peace. But sleep itself, the blessed state, is absent from his plays. Literature here has found its object and makes no effort to encompass that which does not come naturally to it. Do Viola or Prospero, Iago or Coriolanus ever sleep? Will they ever sleep? We cannot imagine it.

As you see, my dear, I am writing anything that comes to mind, partly out of the hope that in that way I will find a path that leads me out of my dilemma, partly in order to put off the moment when I will have to face it head on. I little thought, as I drove here yesterday with our friend Hammond, that it would come to this. But it has. The broad vista has become a high wall that prevents me advancing, and nothing I do seems capable of helping me find a way round or over it. The clock ticks away and I still sit here writing to you, as though it would be nothing to invent a story to do the trick. As though, even, I could go to him empty-handed and trust my inspiration to carry me through the next few hours.

For a moment I thought I had it. I thought I would write my piece for him in the form of a letter to you, in which I would recount my day and then tell you of the dilemma I faced and of my failure to comply with his demands. I thought, in my folly, that this admission would itself be the story, that my recognition of my failure would be my ultimate success. But though that seemed a sort of solution when I was engaged on it, I have since come to feel that it is no solution at all. Since then I have sat here daydreaming, while time has ticked away.

Are the excuses formulated nothing more than just that, excuses for my gross inadequacy? I do not think so. In fact I know that this is not the case. And yet I find no way to justify myself when faced with Westfield's simple but devastating question: Why can I not in a day invent something that will satisfy? And if I cannot, is the fault wholly mine?

The truth of the matter is that something deep within me

yearns to be the kind of craftsman he believes me to be, but something else, equally deep, rejects the formulation. But if that is so, why do I still yearn for that other version of myself, why do I still hold up to myself as an ideal the image of the maker, skilled and inventive, capable of coping with every challenge?

It seems so long since I arrived here, yesterday afternoon, intrigued by my commission, curious about the house and its owner, my heart suffused, as always, with love of you, and never doubting my ability to do what I had been asked. Now it feels as though it was only on arrival here that I really began to live, that all my life until that moment had been a happy dream, like the dream of childhood. I think that if I did not have your image always before me to keep me going, did not, quite simply, have you to write to, I would shrivel up and disappear. But I think of you and feel I have to fight my way through this for your sake. And yet if I did not have you would I feel so desperate? Would I not simply make my excuses and leave? If I did not have you of course I would not be myself but someone else, someone without substance and without purpose, without a role and without feelings. I look for this person and know he exists, that he is not so very different from the person who, in his misguided integrity, refuses to comply with the demands made upon him by Westfield. It frightens me to admit this, but perhaps that is the person I have been discovering myself to be in these last few hours, as I have sat here writing to you. I can imagine myself now getting up from this table, packing my things, making my excuses, and departing. But not in order to return home. For that person has no home to return to. Not in order to come back to you and the house, to my wife and my children and my animals, but rather to wander out into the world, alone and invisible, without a place to rest his head, without skills, without even a language to speak. I cannot think what would become of such a person, but for the first time I can imagine such a fate for myself.

The thought of packing my bag and leaving this house for ever, of vanishing into the world without a sound, like a drop of water added to a stream, fills me with a curious excitement. I do not know what will happen to me, but it no longer seems to matter. The need to disappear is taking hold of me and will not let me go.

Will you be able to understand? Will you be able to conceive of the possibility of my returning one day? To be honest, I cannot conceive of it, it seems to me that as the drop at once blends with the stream and disappears for ever, so, once I have left this cursed house, I too will disappear, even to myself. But as I sit here now, writing this letter to you which I have still not decided whether to leave for you or to burn, I still have not merged and so I still, in one corner of my being, hope and believe that we will one day come together again.

It is all so sudden that I hardly know what I am doing. Certainly when I began this letter I had no idea that this was where it would lead me. Soon, though, my bag will be packed and I will be able to slip out without anyone noticing, leaving nothing behind me except, perhaps, this letter. Now I know my destiny I realise that I have perhaps always known it, that I have perhaps been waiting for this moment all my life. Our ancestors, after all, have always been wanderers, that is perhaps why our laws have made so much of binding us into family and community – for fear that the atavistic desire to let go, to leave everything behind us as Abraham left everything behind him, might at any time get the better of us.

It has grown dark as I have been writing. Soon I will depart. I have decided to leave this letter here on the desk in an envelope addressed to you. To him I will say nothing. I am greatly relieved to be free of him, to be free of the burden of pretence that has characterised our relationship since I first arrived. Let him find another magician to work his spells upon him – and even if he fails to do so, even if he never has a sound night's sleep again, let that be his fate and let him embrace it with the courage and resourcefulness with which we, each of us, have to embrace our fate.

I must stop – and yet I am reluctant to stop. It is as though this letter were my lifeline to you and to the self I am and have been for so long. When I put the last full stop to it and sign it that will be the end. But of course what I have learned in the past few hours is that I have never been who and what I thought I was and that therefore leaving this behind is a necessary step.

I have been walking up and down in the gathering gloom for several minutes, and then standing at the long window, looking out at the trees. You will hardly believe this, but as I stood there I almost came to the conclusion that what I have been writing here is nonsense, a wild dream of flight, an evasion of responsibility, brought on by Westfield's ultimatum. What had seemed so clear only a few minutes ago seemed suddenly murky and confused. I even thought of sitting down again at the desk and writing the narrative Westfield asked of me, tearing up this letter and never breathing a word to you or anyone else about the crisis that has so suddenly come upon me in this room. But then that thought too passed away and I saw it for what it was: a last moment of weakness, a last clinging to the old ways. Now I am strong again. Now I am ready to do what has to be done. Goodbye, my darling, goodbye, and God bless you now and for ever.

25. The Postcard

I sit at my desk, the postcard propped in front of me. It is many nights now since I have been able to sleep. Not a word from Edith. But I can do without her. I have my book to finish. Until it is done I know I will have no rest. But the cause of my sleeplessness is not that I am driven to express what I have in my head. I wish that were so, but it is not. The cause of my sleeplessness is, rather, that I am racked by doubts about whether there is any point in expressing anything. Racked by doubts? What exactly does that mean? Why, when things start to go wrong, do the clichés begin to proliferate? Begin to proliferate? No, no. That way madness lies.

Start again.

When I am working well, when I am on the right track, I sleep like a log. It is only when nothing advances any more and I can see no way forward and I cannot even see why there should be a way forward that I find it impossible to sleep. And when I cannot sleep I cannot work. It's as simple as that. When I cannot work I cannot sleep and when I cannot sleep I cannot work. Hey ho.

I was wrong to blame Edith, though she is not entirely without responsibility. But the book was sunk long before Colmar. It was sunk the moment I started it. It never had a chance. I don't know why I ever set out on that impossible journey in the first place. What have I to do with Goldberg, Westfield, Ballantyne and the rest? What do I know about England or Scotland in the year 1800, or about the Jews of that time or the landed gentry? Why should I want to tell these stories and to tell them in this way?

I have tried putting them aside and turning to something

nearer home, but I hate to leave a job uncompleted once I have begun it, and I soon found I could not concentrate on anything else. I was eager to go back to Goldberg, Westfield and the rest. So I did.

Yet I cannot complete it.

I cannot leave it and I cannot complete it.

I sit at my desk and wonder whether my disillusionment with the whole project is only the result of my own inadequacy. Wonder for the umpteenth time. Have I missed something? Was there a turning I should have taken? Or should I simply grit my teeth and keep going? Is this, in other words, simply the kind of crisis of confidence that attacks one in the middle of every major project, or is it a clear sign that the project itself was flawed from the start?

There was a time when I would take books home from the library and sit down to read them with excitement: books about England in the reign of George III, books about the archaeology of Orkney and the Wild Boy of Aveyron, books by contemporary novelists whose aims at first blush seemed to parallel my own. These, I thought, would show me how to proceed. But they never did. None of them seemed to have anything to do with my project and so they held no interest for me at all. Soon I gave up reading altogether. Now I cannot write and I cannot read. I cannot write because I do not know how to go on, and I cannot read because without something to go on there seems little point in reading anything. I cannot get drunk because my liver is in a terrible state and I cannot watch TV because after an hour or two my eyes start to hurt. I cannot get to sleep because my mind keeps returning to the intractable problems of the book and so when I get up in the morning I feel exhausted and never during the whole day do I feel properly awake. All in all a pretty pass.

Edith said to me when I showed her the first: Write another twenty-nine. That is all you have to do. To keep me interested for twenty-nine more train journeys, she said. And so I went on. A part of me wished simply to keep her amused. But a part of me knew too that she had used the word 'interested', and that that was very different from the word 'amused'. To be interested you have to feel that something genuine is being addressed. You have to feel that more is at stake than the skilful telling of thirty anec-dotes. You have to feel that each is valid in itself and yet that all will add up to more than the sum of the parts.

I look at the postcard propped on my desk: the signature, *Klee*, in his expressive hand, just below the roughly painted-in-frame, then, below that, '1940 L13 Wander-Artist (ein Plakat)'. On the back it says that it is a 'peinture à la colle sur papier brouillon collé sur carton [31 × 29 cm.] coll privée – Suisse'. I know that this is what I need to capture. It looks simple. And yet.

I had thought that talking about myself would validate the rest, would give it grounding, authority. But the figure mocks me, telling me that this is a mistake. Perhaps, though, it is a mistake I have to make. In the silence of the night, as I look back over the bits of Bach and Hölderlin and Klee that go to make up this pecu-liar book, I have to accept that what I feel about Edith or whether I can sleep or not is of no interest to anyone but myself. And yet I know too that without this confession of failure I would not be able to go on.

But I cannot go on. In my desperation I turned Goldberg out of the house, sent him forth into the silence of exile. It was, on my part, nothing less than a form of suicide. Or, to be less melo-dramatic, nothing less than the recognition that I had come to the end myself. I am sick of this absurd charade, of this costume drama with only fragments of costume still clinging like seaweed to the bodies. Perhaps that is the costume drama of the future. I doubt it. Or, if it is, it is not for me.

I look at the postcard again and for the first time I am struck by an anomaly. The *Wander-Artist*, Klee called it. But why, if the title is in English, does the description of what it is (ein Plakat) follow in German? I look up *plakat* in the dictionary and find that it means a bill, a placard or poster. What exactly is a placard? I look that up in the *Shorter OED*. Here it is, under 1:2: 'A notice, or other document, printed on one side of a single sheet, to be posted up, or otherwise publicly displayed; a bill, a poster 1560.'

So, Klee intends this to be or to give the appearance of being, a document to be posted up in public places, an advertisement for something, in other words. But for what? And does the term *wander-artist* mean something other in German than it does in

English? I suddenly wonder. My dictionary (Cassell) gives nothing under the hyphenated form, but has entries under both *wander* and *artist*: '*Wander*, v.: travel (on foot), go, walk, wander, ramble, hike, roam.' As an adjective: 'itinerant, strolling, nomadic.' So a *wander-arbeitung* is an itinerant worker. As for *artist*, the only synonym it gives is 'artiste'. What exactly does that word mean? The *Shorter OED* is not very helpful: 'One who makes his craft a "fine art"... One skilled in a. music; b. dramatic art.' The *OED* proper is more helpful: 'artiste: a public performer who appeals to the aesthetic faculties, as a professional singer, dancer, etc.: also: one who makes "fine art" of his employment, as an artistic cook, hairdresser, etc.'

So there we have it: a *wander-artist* is not a wandering artist but an itinerant public performer, an itinerant actor or even a con-man like Autolycus in *The Winter's Tale*. The *wander-artist* is coming to town and up go the posters. That, at least, is Klee's conceit, when he painted this, in the last year of his life and the first year of the war.

I look at the postcard again and find I take heart from it. This was perhaps the place where I had to emerge. Now I have done so I can disappear and perhaps the work can go on. But I doubt it.

26. Between

He sits with his head in his hands. He does not know how much time has gone by, for his heart is heavy. It had all begun so well, with such excitement, such a feeling of doors opening, new worlds to be conquered. But gradually, over the months and years, his mood has changed. At first he tried to shut out the doubts, to convince himself that they were merely the result of his natural tiredness, of the inevitable fading of the initial euphoria. But now he has finally to face the fact that he cannot go on, that his inspiration has abandoned him and the idea alone cannot carry him forward. Once more, as so often before, he has had to ask himself whether this is because of some failure in himself or because the project itself was flawed and should never have been persisted with. And, as so often before, he has had to admit that he does not know.

He has been over this ground so many times that even the setting forth of his doubts now feels stale and abstract. Yet it is not as though there were other lines of thought which felt fresher to him. No. All feels flat, hollow, there is no way out in that direction, but there is no other direction left to follow.

He returns to what he has achieved so far. And there he has to admit that his failure is even more comprehensive than he had thought. These figures he has created, tried to breathe life into, have very little credibility. His sense of the period is weak, some of the events he has tried to invoke smell vaguely of the eighteenth, others of the nineteenth century. Certain events, such as the discovery of the village of Skara Brae in Orkney, did not occur till the 1850s, while others, such as the capture of the Wild Boy of

Aveyron, date back to the 1790s. He has tried to set a world in motion and all he has done is reveal the paucity of his mind and the cardboard nature of his creatures.

He has tried to enliven things by inventing a present-day figure through which to filter the rest, but far from this giving authenticity to the work, it has only made it seem contrived and false, though some of the details, such as Leila Haverkampf's gesture of simultaneously pushing the little glasses up her nose and sweeping her hair out of her eyes, have given him momentary pleasure. He has tried to ground the whole by finally speaking in the first person, but that first person seems as false and hollow as the rest and he has quickly discarded it. Why did he ever set out on this road? He does not know. Something has driven him forward, until the weight of reality, the reality of the past, the reality of the present, have finally brought him to a stop.

He recognises his weariness by the staleness of his language. Where is the old excitement? Where is the feeling that once accompanied every venture into fiction? And again the question: Is it that he has simply run out of steam, chosen the wrong form, or is this sense of weariness, this sense of emptiness, itself something to be examined, to be explored, to be written about, a fact of life like sexual desire and ageing and death? Once, he feels, he would have known instinctively, not now.

And yet is that 'not now' not perhaps itself of interest, itself what needs to be explored? The same old question, the same old lack of an answer.

To return to what he has been trying to do. It is not just that he has failed to convince, that he has not done adequately what he set out to do. It is, he realises, that he has not done it adequately because he was never wholly convinced in the first place that it should be done at all. For what have they to do with him, these wolf boys, these Skara Braes, these country houses with their great parks, these quarrels between husbands and wives, these holidays in Switzerland and meetings with collectors? They are far far away from his own life and his own concerns, from his own needs and his own desires.

– But then what is near? the other asks him.

– Near? he says, looking up in surprise.

– What is near? the other asks again.

– Near to my life? To my own needs and desires?

– Exactly.

– I don't know, he has to confess. And then, in a violent outburst:

– Not that. At any rate not that.

– Ask yourself what is, the other says, smiling.

– I ask, he says, but I cannot answer.

– Perhaps, the other says, what is near can only be arrived at by talking about what is far away.

– I had thought of that, he says, but it does not help.

– You had not thought enough, the other says.

– How does one think enough? he asks, smiling in his turn.

– Where will you go? the other asks. If you renounce this, where will you go?

– I don't know, he confesses.

– You don't know, the other repeats. Then, as he is silent, adds: – Perhaps it is not the details that count, although every story is made up of details, but something else.

– What? he asks.

– That which lies in between, for example, the other says. In between the details and in between the different stories. Perhaps you have lost heart because you have lost the ability to recognise the importance of between.

– Of course, he goes on, such loss of confidence is almost inevitable, for if you could see the importance of between it would no longer be between and so would no longer be what is important.

– Between, the other goes on, is only a way of talking. It is perhaps only a way of talking about time. Time the healer, not time the destroyer. Only another way of asking you to trust in time, in the time of working and the time of reading.

– But how can I trust in time when nothing that is done by me has the quality of authenticity?

– You and your questions, the other says. I have told you. Between is only a way of talking. What is important is not to be found in any place and it is not to be found in any time, either the time before you began or the time after you have finished. It is not inside anything or outside anything, but is what has made these things happen. Do you understand me?

– Perhaps I am beginning to, he says, smiling at the other's smile.

– What makes and has made these marks is not you, the other goes on, and it is not not you.

– Who is it then? he asks.

– Can you not guess? the other asks, his smile widening.

– You?

The other does not answer but goes on smiling, so that gazing at him fills him with joy, and this time the joy does not evaporate but seems to grow until it fills the entire room and the sky outside and the air, it fills the trees and envelopes the birds swooping past the window, it reverberates through the room so that it is something tangible, he feels he can reach out his hand and touch it, and, feeling that, accepts that the other is no longer there and has dissolved into those vibrations, into the trees and sky.

Now the hands no longer clasp the head, the eyes no longer close in resignation. I am on my way.   ▌

27. Wander-Artist

Here I am, one hand raised in mock salute, on my way to the other side.

The other side of what?

It does not matter. The other side.

I have perhaps come from somewhere and I am going somewhere else, but in the mean time here I am, one arm raised, on my way.

It does not matter where I have come from. You could say that I am only alive when I come into view and where I am going is anyone's guess.

I arrived with Goldberg and where I am going is anyone's guess. I was present with Westfield and when I leave he will be no more.

Is someone after me? Am I in pursuit of another? Not that I know, but then I know very little. The one who chases may feel he will catch me, but he is mistaken. The one who flees may feel I will catch him, but he is mistaken. Without me there would be no Goldberg and there would be no Westfield, but then without them I would not exist either. Look at me hard and I vanish before your eyes; ignore me and I will have my revenge.

Who am I? Where do I come from? Nobody knows. Where am I going? Nobody knows. I am on my way and only the most foolish would pretend that I do not exist.

Why Goldberg? Why Westfield? Nobody knows. Why Ballantyne? Why Hammond? Nobody knows.

Without me all is heavy, sluggish, dead. With me all comes alive and starts to dance. Do not ask who I am or all will shatter and collapse and darkness take the place of light.

A little corner of the world. Of a world which never existed and is not exactly an invention either. I am witness to that.

To put it another way: If I was not here, passing through, there would be either the dead weight of history or the dead weight-lessness of pure invention. I am passing through: Pay attention and you may catch a glimpse of me.

Men and women in factories and offices, in fields and studies, in schoolrooms and hospital wards. All these know I am passing but are too weary to lift their heads. If they would only do so they would see my face, my upraised arm, and they would return my greeting.

I am on my way. Something has caused me to leave home and set out, but I do not wish to know what. I am content to be on my way. Something awaits me when I have passed across but I do not trouble myself with asking what. It is enough that I am in motion, passing through the world.

The world? What world? The world you thought you knew buckles as I pass and reforms in unexpected way. That is not the world you knew, but then neither is the world about you. If it could have been this way then it needn't have been that, but it had to be some way.

You do not listen to what I say. You are too busy watching me cross over, one arm raised in salute. And that is as it should be, for what I say has no significance, I cannot even be said to say it, only to mouth the words of others, and what you have heard you have not really heard, what you have seen you have not really seen. Yet here I am, on my way, arm raised in greeting, and then I am no more.

28. The Offering

My dear. It is done. He is asleep. I have accomplished what I was asked here to do and I am very tired.

It seems so long ago that I left home. I am longing to return and see you and the children. I am very tired.

I cannot tell you how hard I have worked in these last two days. How many stories I have constructed and taken apart again and constructed once more and then discarded and then resurrected only to discard once again. I had not imagined it would entail so much. There were times when I was more than willing to give up. When my mind refused to function and my hand to form the letters.

I never thought it would be easy, but in the event I was pushed almost beyond my powers.

I know you will understand. You have seen me at work. And though this was harder than anything I have ever done, it was, I suppose, not essentially different.

And yet at times it felt as though the effort would cut me off from you for ever. As though it was taking me into an unknown realm from which I would never be able to find my way back.

At times I thought this place was under a spell, that I was one of those old knights who comes to an enchanted castle and there is forced to undergo trials of which he had never dreamed, and some of which he is not even aware he is undergoing, in order to bring the old king back to life or to wake the sleeping princess. I thought at times that I would be transformed, as Odysseus' companions were transformed by the witch-goddess Circe.

And in a sense I have been. For I have changed a great deal in the course of the past two days. Those hours of concentration at my desk, those strange conversations with Mr Westfield in the dark, the magic of the great park at dawn and dusk, have all made my old self, the self who kissed you goodbye, the self who got into Hammond's carriage only two days ago, fade away like a ghost or a mirage. He paid me well, but what I did for him was beyond all payment. For the price he exacted, or rather the price I paid, was nothing less than the offering of my whole self.

Do you understand what I am saying? I do not expect you to, for I can hardly do so myself. When I set out all was clear. I was a certain sort of person with a certain sort of life behind me, and I was going to undertake a certain sort of task for a certain sort of patron. But in the course of my stay here I have changed as much as he has. Only you have remained constant. I wonder if that constancy and my change will not have altered our relationship for ever.

I do not know what I am saying. I am so tired. At moments I think you will understand me perfectly, that you do understand me perfectly, and at others that you will not understand me at all. If, that is, I decide to send this. And if it arrives before I do. Or if, arriving first, I allow you to read it when it arrives in its turn.

The phrase *das Opfer* means in German not just 'the offering' but also 'the sacrifice', and in particular the supreme sacrifice, Christ's offering of his body to redeem mankind. I thought of that tonight as we talked in the dark, Westfield and I, and thought that my own offering to him was perhaps analogous. I do not mean to be blasphemous, but the feeling was very strong that I was in some sense offering my own body so as to release his. What I had written and read was not simply a well-made piece of work designed to perform the function required of it, none of the work I have made to order has ever been less than that, but in the longer perspective it was a kind of offering of myself on some sort of altar, not a Christian offering of course, nor a Jewish one, but something else, something which can be hinted at in Christian terms, but which remains itself without words and without images or any narrative that could explain it.

I think you will understand. I think when it is all over – but what do I mean by 'all over'? – it will shine forth like a bright star in the heavens, even if and when I am no longer there.

It is very early in the morning, my dear, and I have had no sleep all night. Perhaps this explains the strange state I am in and the oddity of this letter. I know you are there and will always be there, whatever happens to me.

The whole house is asleep around me. As if I had waved a wand and put it to sleep. As if it too would never wake up.

And me? Am I awake or have I too fallen asleep and am writing this to you in my dreams? I do not know and it no longer seems very important. It is as though I had left my body there in that room, sleeping on that bed, and were now free but also lost.

I know that is how I always feel when I have finished an appointed task. Until the next task is started I do not feel I exist, I do not feel I have a body. But this time it is different. It is as though I sense that I will not start again, that all that is over for good. And that allows me to talk about it with an ease I have never felt before, in this letter to you which is perhaps not a letter at all.

I think of you now and know you are thinking of me and the thought gives me strength. It allows me to see the desk at which I am sitting and the page, lit by two candles, on which I am writing. But it does not seem to be my hand which is writing, or indeed any hand at all. The words appear on the page before me and I watch them as they form. But it is not I who form them.

I am very tired. I am very sleepy. It is all over. Not one world but a multitude of worlds have come into being and then passed away since I kissed you goodbye and got into Hammond's carrriage. I see them like those coloured bubbles we used to blow as children, which floated off into the breeze and then in an instant burst and vanished. So many bubbles. So many worlds. And ours only one of them. The thought causes me no anguish, not even any sadness. On the contrary, I feel a sort of elation as I watch the bubbles float and burst, each in turn, in the clear night air. And at the back of everything is the sense that you will be waiting for me, whenever I come home, to whatever home I come. Yes. You will be waiting.

29. For You Alone

In the late afternoon of July 19, 18—, the novelist and poet Samuel Goldberg arrived at Somerton Hall, in the county of B—, the home of Tobias Westfield Esq. It was a fine summer's day and the birds were in full song.

– Welcome! said the footman as he held the carriage door open.

– Welcome! said the butler as they stepped inside the house.

– Welcome! said the housekeeper, and curtsied to him on the stairs.

– Your room, Mr Goldberg, said the maid as she opened the door.

Goldberg was enchanted by the large bright room. Catching sight of a vase of flowers on the table he thought: What beautiful flowers!

– Mr Westfield thought you might like to rest before dinner sir, said the maid, who had followed him into the room.

Beautiful! thought Goldberg again, and turned to her.

– Did you pick them yourself? he asked her.

– No sir, but I arranged them in the vase.

– My wife couldn't have done better, Goldberg said. And she has a way with flowers.

He bent over the vase, endeavouring to smell each bloom.

– Dinner is at eight, sir, the maid said, and stepped out of the room, closing the door soundlessly behind her.

Goldberg went to the window and threw it open. Birdsong filled the room.

He sat in the window seat and looked out over the kitchen garden at the tall trees of the park beyond.

*

The dinner bell found him walking up and down the room, dressed and hungry.

There was a knock on the door and the footman was standing there when he opened it.

– I will convey you to dinner sir, he said.

– Thank you, Goldberg said, and followed him

The company was assembled in the drawing-room, whose French windows were open onto the terrace. As soon as Goldberg entered, Westfield came towards him, hands outstretched:

– Welcome! he said. He took Goldberg's hand and held it between both of his for an instant, looking into his face as though searching for something. Then he led him forward and introduced him to the company: Dr and Mrs Carpenter, Mr and Mrs Ballantyne, a lady whose name he did not catch, and the two sons, the elder with his tutor and the younger with a governess: Mr Pennyquick and Miss Lamond, Goldberg thought he heard.

– You must be hungry after your long journey, Westfield said. Let us proceed to dinner without further ado.

He led the way into the dining-room. Goldberg blinked at the vision of silver and crystal.

– Let us be seated, Westfield said. We do not stand upon ceremony in this house.

He himself sat down at the head of the table, with his elder son at the other end. On his right sat the nameless lady, with Goldberg next to her and Mrs Carpenter on his other side. Next to her sat Ballantyne, with the elder boy on his right and the tutor opposite him. The younger child sat between the tutor and the governess. Next to her sat Dr Carpenter, with Mrs Ballantyne between him and their host.

Westfield rang a little bell and then turned to Goldberg:

– It is most kind of you to come all this way, Mr Goldberg, he said.

– I am delighted to be here, Goldberg said.

– This calls for a little celebration, Westfield said, and raised his glass. All followed suit.

– It does indeed, said the lady on Goldberg's left. It does indeed. The meal was now served.

– It is curious, Westfield said to Goldberg, but when you entered just now I could have sworn I had seen you before.

– Really? Goldberg said.

– How could that be? Westfield said. Have our paths crossed before, Mr Goldberg?

– Not to my knowledge, Goldberg said.

– Strange, Westfield said. I could have sworn it.

He bent over his plate and Goldberg did likewise.

– You have come from far, Mr Goldberg? the doctor's wife asked him.

– A fair distance, Goldberg said.

– Mr Goldberg has come to read to me, Westfield said smiling. He has come to send me to sleep.

– We are aware of that, the lady sitting between them said. You have been talking of little else this past month.

– My father is a faddist, the elder son said.

– Come come, Ballantyne said. That is hardly complimentary to your father or to Mr Goldberg.

– I was merely stating a fact, the elder son said.

They ate in silence.

– Cabbages and kings, Goldberg said.

– I beg your pardon? said Westfield.

– Cabbages, Goldberg said. And kings.

– Ah, Westfield said.

– And which are you? the elder son said.

– Which?

– A cabbage or a king?

– Which would you say? asked Goldberg.

– Let us drink to your arrival, Westfield said.

All drank.

– We have heard, Ballantyne said, how you were received at court.

Goldberg bowed his head.

– Your skills, Mr Goldberg, Mrs Ballantyne said, are legendary.

– Are you a miracle worker? the elder son asked.

– Neither a miracle worker nor a water diviner, Goldberg said. I am a humble author.

– Let us drink to the success of our venture, Westfield said.

They drank.

– Are you married, Mr Goldberg? asked the unknown lady.

– I am, Madam.

– And you have children?

– I do.

– Are you proud of your children?

– Inordinately, Goldberg said.

– That is the prerogative of fathers, the elder son said.

– Cat! the younger one cried. He struggled to get out of his chair. The young governess restrained him. Cat! he cried again.

– Let me introduce you to our cat, Westfield said.

– What is his name? asked Goldberg.

– He doesn't have a name, the elder son said.

– He has a most remarkable ability to dance, Westfield said to Goldberg.

– Really? Goldberg said.

– Listen, Westfield said. Look.

He tapped his knife against the glass. The ginger cat rose on his hind legs and waved his arms in the air.

The assembled company sat in silence, watching him.

– May I? Goldberg said.

He pushed back his chair and stood up. He sank to his knees and advanced on the cat, following the animal's movements with his own. 'The huge mighty oaks themselves did advance,' he intoned, 'and leaped from the hills to learn for to dance.'

– 'The huge mighty oaks themselves did advance,' bellowed the elder child, banging his knife against his glass, 'and leapt from the hills to learn for to dance!'

Westfield stood up and bowed to the unknown lady. She in her turn stood up and together they began to waltz round the table.

'The huge mighty oaks themselves did advance, and leapt from the hills to learn for to dance!' sang Goldberg, and soon Ballantyne and Mrs Carpenter, old Dr Carpenter and Mrs Ballantyne, the young governess and the tutor, and the two boys were all dancing round the table, while Goldberg, on his knees, swayed in unison with the ginger cat. 'The huge mighty oaks themselves did advance, and leapt from the hills to learn for to dance!' sang the company.

'My bonny lies over the ocean, My bonny lies over the sea, My bonny lies over the ocean, Oh bring back my bonny to me!' sang Westfield. 'Bring back, bring back, Oh bring back my bonny to me!' sang the children. 'Bring back, bring back, Oh bring back my bonny to me, to me!' sang the rest of the company.

Westfield clapped his hands.

– Enough! he said.

Goldberg, who had been prancing round the table with the younger child on his shoulders, handed him back to his governess. The tutor wiped his moustache with the middle fingers of both hands. Westfield patted his forehead with his handkerchief.

– I will see you in my room at eleven, Westfield said to Goldberg. James will show you the way.

Ballantyne shook Goldberg's hand.

– It's been a pleasure to meet you, sir, he said.

– I'm sorry we didn't have the chance to talk at greater length, the unknown lady said to him.

– I wish you the best of luck, the elder son said.

*

At the appointed hour the footman led Goldberg through the great house to his master's rooms. Westfield was in the antechamber, pouring himself a glass of something golden.

– A drop for you? he asked.

– Thank you, Goldberg said.

Handing him his glass, Westfield said again: – I'm sure we've met somewhere before.

Goldberg shrugged.

– Well, Westfield said, holding out his own glass, here's to your very good health.

– And to yours, Goldberg said, raising his in turn.

Westfield swallowed his drink in one gulp and put the empty glass down on the table.

– Are you ready? he asked.

– Of course.

– Then I shall get into bed.

– Remember, Goldberg said. Cabbages and kings.

– I won't forget.

Goldberg sat down in the chair indicated to him in the antechamber, while his host withdrew into the bedroom, which was in darkness.

Goldberg pulled a sheaf of papers from his jacket pocket and tapped them into a neat pile on his knees.

– Shall I begin, sir? he enquired.

– When you are ready, Mr Goldberg, when you are ready.

Slowly then, in his warm, mellifluous voice, Goldberg began to read.

30. The Final Fugue

Mr Samuel Goldberg, the novelist and poet, arrived at the country residence of Mr Tobias Westfield rather earlier than expected. Bidding goodbye to his friend Richard Hammond, in whose carriage he had made the journey, he swung his bag over his shoulder and stood for a moment on the steps leading to the front door. The coachman urged the horses forward and the carriage swung away, slowly gathering speed as it went.

Goldberg, looking up, caught a glimpse of Hammond's white face in the window and thought he saw a hand raised in parting salute.

Acknowledgements

Chapter 5 consists of extracts from W.Douglas Simpson, *The Ancient Stones of Scotland*, Robert Hale, London, 1965; further extracts are used in Chapter 7.

Chapters 13 and 14 incorporate several poems of Hölderlin, in the translation by Michael Hamburger, *Hölderlin*, The Harvill Press, London, 1952. For Chapter 13 I have also drawn on David Constantine's *Hölderlin*, The Clarendon Press, Oxford, 1988, and Georg Büchner's *Lenz*.